The Theme Park at the End of the World

Also by Eric R. Asher

Shop ebooks, audiobooks, and paperbacks at
ericrasherstore.com

The Theme Park at the End of the World

The Steamborn Series

Steamborn

Steamforged

Steamsworn

Skyborn

Skyforged

Skysworn

Stormborn

Stormforged

Stormsworn

The Vesik Series
(Recommended for Ages 17+)

Days Gone Bad

Wolves and the River of Stone

Winter's Demon

This Broken World

Destroyer Rising

Rattle the Bones

Witch Queen's War

Forgotten Ghosts

The Book of the Ghost

The Book of the Claw

The Book of the Sea
The Book of the Staff
The Book of the Rune
The Book of the Sails
The Book of the Wing
The Book of the Blade
The Book of the Fang
The Book of the Reaper
Dreams of the Forgotten Dead
Garden Gnome Graves

The Vesik Series Box Sets

Box Set One (Books 1-3)
Box Set Two (Books 4-6)
Box Set Three (Books 7-8)
Box Set Four: The Books of the Dead Part 1
Box Set Five: The Books of the Dead Part 2

Mason Dixon: Monster Hunter

Episode One
Episode Two
Episode Three
Episode Four

Want to receive an email when one of Eric's books releases?
Visit ericrasher.com to get started.

The Theme Park at the End of the World

Eric R. Asher

Dedicated to some of my favorite vloggers. Molly, Alan, Max, Jackie, Sam, Anna, Tyler, Taylor, and Nate.

Thanks for keeping us all connected to the parks when we can't be there.

Mammoth Club

Super Enthused

Expedition Theme Park

The Pugh Two

Orlando Informer

Paging Mr. Morrow

For those we lost. I wish we could ride together one last time.

DARK FOREST
10 GOWROW'S CAVE
11 THE MINE

MERROWS LAGOON
5 THE BLACK KETTLE BAKERY
6 PEDAL BOATS
7 MERROWS FEAST
8 OCEAN TREASURES
9 KRAKEN'S FURY

FAERIE
1 DUBLIN STREET
2 CELTIC FAIR SOUVENIRS
3 FAERIE GLEN
4 THE GRAND THEATRE

LOST EMPIRE
12 PUFFING DEMONS
13 AIRSHIPS
14 TINKER'S ESCAPE
15 POTATO on a STICK

HOWLING MOUNTAIN
16 TREASURES of VALHALLA
17 NORDIC EATS
18 TREASURE of TROLL PEAKS
19 ODIN'S HALL
20 THE BOBSLED

CARNIVAL
21 BOARDWALK GAMES
22 MONSTER MOUSE
23 PRETZELS
24 WHIMSY CAROUSEL

HR
DARK FOREST
LOST EMPIRE
TITANIA'S TABLE
MERROWS LAGOON
HOWLING MOUNTAIN
CARNIVAL
FAERIE
FUTURE COASTER
THE THEME PARK AT THE END OF THE WORLD
N E S W

Chapter 1

ELLIE SMILED AND walked through the queue for her favorite ride. It didn't matter how many times she'd been on it, or the strange looks she got from some of her coworkers for staying after her shift to enjoy the short lines. Without the crowds, she could stop and look at every detail she wanted, from the old tinker's workshop filled with gadgets and puffs of steam to the crumbling walls of a mountain city that looked real enough to fool any historian.

"Ellie, wait up!"

She turned to find Cole speed walking through the queue behind her, tufts of sandy brown hair sticking out of his hoodie. He was late again, which wasn't anything unusual, but he was often on time for night rides.

"What happened?" Ellie asked.

"Roman." Cole rolled his eyes as if that one name answered everything. And in many ways, it did.

"What now?"

"Something about new food to try?" Cole clenched his fists before rubbing the back of his hand. "I don't know. I tuned it all out once Hans got excited about the idea of serving some weird Nordic cheese on pretzels."

Ellie led the way into the next room as she pondered what kind of cheese Cole counted as weird. The thought lingered as she studied the décor there, filled with the glint of giant spider eyes in the darkness, which unsettled many of the guests. Her heart leapt when the sound of the launch echoed through the hall, the buzz of wheels on a track rising to a roar. They were close now.

Cole sighed as they stepped into the station of Tinker's Escape. "None of the other coasters get to me. Why am I still nervous about this thing?"

"Because it's one of the best roller coasters in the park? Certainly, the best ride in Lost Empire."

"I mean, the only other rides in the land are the old cars and the stunningly named Airships."

Ellie laughed. "It's still one of my favorite sections of the park. But you're right about Airships. Who thought to give the name Airships to a slow blimp ride? One that just rises into the air for maybe five minutes? At least the theming is good."

They'd only have to wait for two of the sleek trains—painted in shades of copper and brass with pipes and pistons along the sides—to cycle through before they'd get to ride. Short lines were the best lines. Ellie grinned at the returning trains, cheers and joy and shock plastered across the various faces. Cole fell silent as the next train launched, slipping through the tunnel to the preshow. He took a deep breath and blew it out slowly, likely realizing they'd scored the first row. That was enough to make anyone nervous, or very excited.

Their train rolled into the station, slowing gradually to a stop before the lap bars released with a clunk. The restraints rose over the riders' heads before they slid out the opposite side. The gates opened, and Ellie hopped up into the seat and pulled the bar down. She much preferred the deep seats and lack of shoulder restraints to the Gowrow's Cave coaster across the park.

Ride ops started down either side, dressed in leather aprons and decked out with pistons and working gears on their forearms. They checked to make sure each lap bar was properly secured as everyone got settled. With that done and a thumbs up thrown, the train lurched forward to what doubled as an on-ride preshow and safety spiel.

The room looked much like the tinker's workshop from the queue, but larger, with a sliding door off to the side that shook and appeared ready to splinter as some unseen force pounded on it. The boom alone was intimidating in that space, but the ride ops added so much more.

Kevin ran onto the scene in chunky, ancient-looking boots. Tall and lanky and fully geared up in a leather apron weighed down with tools, he gestured wildly to the guests as the train slowed to a stop. "You all made it this far! Can you hear them? The guards are getting close now. Keep your fingers and anything else you'd like to keep attached inside the vehicle. Hands up. Head back. Bars down. Hold on to your butts."

Ellie waved at Kevin. "How can we hold on to our butts if we EEEEEeeeeeeeee!"

She caught his smirk as he hit the button for the launch, and Ellie howled with joy as the train shot forward, exchanging the workshop for the absolute darkness of the launch tunnel. The dim flicker of fire to either side gave them the only warning of a turn so sharp it felt like they'd fall out, pinned down only by the lap bars.

Slamming back into their seats, they dove again, only to repeat another intense left turn. The next few elements blurred together, often called a spaghetti bowl, so tangled was the track. Every turn tried to throw them into the air as Ellie reached for the sky, and Cole's knuckles whitened on the lap bar. They soared into another tunnel, a straightaway with guards standing by, swords and halberds outstretched as if to strike down the escapees.

The second launch hit. An explosion of speed shot them all forward, screaming as it slammed them into the side of a top hat, pointing the nose of the train skyward before cresting above the ride's façade, showing them the dying light of sunset over the park before plunging down a near-vertical drop on the other side.

A shallow turn followed, but at speed, it crushed her back into the seat, and Ellie squealed as the track inverted, hanging them upside down for an impossible length of time. The coaster righted them as it dove, jerking them to the side as they entered a tight helix with a pop of airtime.

Another tunnel closed around them, opening into a chasm under the mountain filled with giant creatures, chitinous gleaming limbs and bright eyes reaching out to the tracks ahead of them. The lights dimmed as they reached the first giant bug, then everything went black. Light returned a second later, once they'd passed into a tunnel, revealing the heartline roll they now faced.

Cole shrieked. The countless times they'd ridden it and survived didn't help. The roll always got him.

Ellie laughed and grinned as they rolled. The lap bar caught against their thighs and kept her from a terrible fall before she was upright again, being forced into the bottom of her seat once more.

Two quick turns, and the light of the world vanished into another tunnel, only to open on the brake run as they slid into the finale. A formidable animatronic greeted them: a knight saddled on top of a giant jumping spider. He gestured with his halberd in the mountain cavern.

"You made it, tinkers! Well done. Don't forget to retrieve your loose articles from the lockers. For the Steamsworn!"

"I'm alive again?" Cole clutched his chest as if he didn't quite believe it.

Ellie reached out and patted his knee. "Brave as ever. At least it wasn't the after-hours ride."

Cole's crystal blue and gray eyes widened at the mere suggestion.

They slid back into the station. As soon as the restraints popped open, Ellie pushed up, lifting it back over her head before stepping out. Cole followed, and they headed for the exit.

"Let's go see if Hans has any of that new cheese."

Cole didn't argue.

Ellie stepped onto a winding path, leading them past the boundaries of Lost Empire, where the landscape shifted from dry desert hills into the snowy peaks of Howling Mountain. The soundscaping switched from the rhythmic bursts of steam and gears to the low roar of a mountain wind.

It would have felt ominous if not for the lovely, plucked notes of a lullaby rising and falling like the mountains themselves. They weren't far from Hans there, and unraveling the mystery of his new cheese. Something in the moment filled Ellie with peace. A sweet realization of how lucky she was to work in such a magical place, and how, perhaps more than anything else, she'd never expected to live there.

<h1 align="center">Chapter 2</h1>

ONE OF ELLIE'S favorite things at the park, much to the bafflement of her friends, was the food. Not just any food, but the strange pretzels with a slice of pizza rolled up inside them, and the Tater Tots that never got soggy, no matter how much cheese or pork belly was left to soak into them.

There was the seasonal fare too, which often aligned with some human holiday. It was important to designate them as human, because the man who owned the Theme Park at the End of the World was no man at all. And Ellie was one of the only mortals who knew.

"Ellie."

She jumped at her name, spoken so close to her ear, but she had heard no one approach in the morning sun. She turned to find a tall, slender frame. The kind of visage you might think was fading from some long and terrible illness.

"Are you well?" Roman slowly raised a very fine eyebrow.

"Yes! Sorry. I was just trying the new churro from Hans and couldn't stop staring at the water. Did you need something?" She blinked and frowned at the lake outside Treasure of Troll Peaks.

Roman tapped his chin. "I shall have to revisit that recipe. I would hate to be accused of poisoning my guests."

Ellie's eyes fixated on the churro. She'd only taken a single bite, which didn't make any sense. It was a rare snack that survived long once she got her hands on it. "Wait, you poisoned me?"

"No, of course not. We are not at war." He continued as if that were all the explanation anyone could possibly require. "It has come to my attention that the brownies are somewhat … disgruntled with the current staffing schedule at Treasure of Troll Peaks. They recently doused a rowdy boat of children in honey. Might you reason with them?"

Ellie frowned at the churro she now realized probably had a bit too much magic in it, dropping it into a nearby trashcan, a celebratory shout rising from its depths. She turned her attention back to Roman.

"I'm on it, boss." She gestured toward Nordic Eats, one of the food stands in the distance. "The cheese is good, by the way. The one Hans is putting on flat, crunchy pretzels? I still don't understand how it tastes so much like caramel, but combined with the salt, I love it." She hesitated when she saw the time. "But maybe tone down the churro. I've been pondering existence for thirty minutes!"

She didn't miss his low, peculiar laugh as she walked away, following the crystal-clear water back to the front of the building. Roman appeared again at her side before she rounded the last corner.

"And I would remind you we refer to our Fae foods here as moodscaping."

She turned to tell him what a ridiculous word that was, but he was already gone. "One call to Child Protective Services," Ellie grumbled. "Just one call and I'd never have to hear the word *moodscaping* again."

Now she was annoyed, which put her in the perfect mood to deal with the brownies. That had likely been Roman's plan all along, which annoyed her even more, thus perpetuating the cycle of what many at her old group foster home referred to as "angry Ellie."

From one step to the next, the bright notes of a modern pop song faded, replaced by "In the Hall of the Mountain King." That timeless piece had been the soundtrack for the dark ride as long as Ellie could remember.

A chaotic arrangement of stones formed the foundation of the show building. They had no right to be so stable, propping up the precarious structures of wooden homes with exposed timber lining every inch of the teetering towers. Smoke curled from a few chimneys above.

To any mortal, it would look like nothing more than an artistic feat that formed the façade, the homes in the distance simply a trick of forced perspective. But Ellie knew it was far more than that.

Many of the Fae who worked in the park also lived in those buildings, as did Ellie. While no human soundproofing could have silenced the screams and roars from the dark ride below, magic had far fewer limitations.

Ellie glanced at the sign hanging above the queue, Treasure of Troll Peaks. It wasn't misleading, exactly, but it barely hinted at the adventure inside.

Most humans went in expecting a bit of air conditioning and a slow boat ride. She laughed at that thought and opened the hidden employee door in the wall. The screams hit her first. The kind of half joyous, half terrified sound often reserved for the most intense roller coasters.

Wind whipped at her uniform, bringing a driving rain to accompany the roar of the giant "animatronic" troll.

She kept to the shadows where the water never quite reached. Every time she walked into that space, she remembered Roman's unbridled irritation at a failed inspection by the humans. Once he'd convinced an inspector that some of the most terrifying Fae on that ride were, in fact, animatronics. Well, then the inspectors grew concerned about the clear lack of waterproofing and potential for disaster.

Ellie grinned as a nearby boat lifted gently from the water, its screaming passengers rising high above the narrow trees, their branches curved up as if reaching for the boat.

She continued deeper into the building, passing clusters of clover and the six-petal white blooms of wood anemone.

Beyond those in the meandering stream waited one of the few actual machines inside the show building. A lift fitted with a wide rubber belt, constantly bringing guests up to the second level.

There hadn't always been a second level, but over the years, even the mighty trolls must consider their posture.

A small group of brownies maintained the salvaged lift, long ago rescued from a drowned park in the south of the country.

"Bex!" Ellie called as she mounted the stairs to the structure, hidden by the conical shapes of countless Bells of Ireland flowers, which, of course, had little to do with Ireland itself.

"Bex!"

A pale face under a slouched brown cap peeked over the edge of the stairs.

"Ellie?" Bex's expression turned hard as she squinted at the new arrival. "Did Roman send you?"

Ellie's steps slowed as she reached the top of the lift. "No. He just mentioned you dumped honey on a boat."

Bex blew out a breath and gestured to Ellie. "Come on. We can talk, but until Roman stops allowing three vacations at once, this is going to be hard to maintain."

"Three?" Ellie frowned as she considered that. It took a dozen brownies at minimum to keep all the magic scenes staffed, and if three were on vacation at once …

"Bex, have you been running from scene to scene?"

"Sometimes, yes. We've been taking turns, much like we should be doing with vacation, methinks."

Ellie groaned and slipped into the hidden booth with Bex. "It's Roman who needs to be spoken to, not you."

"Yes." Bex flopped back into the small seat made for her 18-inch form.

Ellie sat in the full-sized office chair beside her, dim monitors casting an eerie glow across the alcove's control console.

She took a deep breath and relaxed in the air conditioning. It was one of the few modern amenities all the Fae enjoyed. Well, all except the gators, but they had their own rides to visit when the season was warm enough.

"So, you heard about the honey?" Bex remained focused on the bank of monitors, her gaze darting to Ellie.

"I heard about the honey, yes."

"You know, not all Fae have infinite patience."

Ellie clutched her chest and gasped. "Everything I know in this world has been a lie."

Bex scowled at her, finally looking away from the screens. "Not all of us enjoy sarcasm, either." But the creases on her forehead lightened as a smile flashed across her face.

"Roman mentioned the staffing schedule has been an issue. Cole and I have been working doubles, too. I'm not excited about it either."

"But you're *humans*. American humans, which means you only exist to brag about how much you work."

Ellie blinked.

"I don't say that to be mean. It's certainly better than the changeling trade from the old days. Stealing people is *definitely* worse than working too much."

"But the schedule?" Ellie hoped the question would focus Bex. The brownie could talk for hours about nothing without a little prompting.

"With four of our crew out and only six left, most of us worked three triple shifts last week." Bex nodded.

Ellie cringed at the idea. A full day shift with human guests, a night shift with the Fae guests, with cleanup and maintenance at the end of it all.

"That's ... awful. Did Roman make them do that?"

Bex hesitated before giving a small shake of her head. "But he didn't stop it, did he? HR is going to kill us all."

The fact the Fae still called cast management HR amused Ellie greatly, as she and Cole were the only humans working at the park. But she didn't feel like smiling about it now.

"Can I talk to Gus about it on your behalf?" Ellie leaned forward as she waited for Bex to decide. Many of the Fae didn't like others speaking for them. Especially human others.

Bex slowly nodded and Ellie felt the tension in her shoulders ease.

"I'll try to get a meeting with the staff together. Between

shifts so it doesn't affect breaks or ride ops, okay?"

"That would be appreciated, Ellie."

She stood to leave. "And if the urge to dump honey on anyone strikes again, maybe ask the crew to stick to water? I'd hate to think what maintenance would have said if that honey had reached the machinery."

Bex shot her a devious grin. "A show, to be sure."

Ellie took the long way out of the ride. She crossed backstage, just out of sight of the boats of guests as they drifted by.

Roman walked a delicate line between making the park a top-tier destination and not arousing suspicion among the humans. But this dark ride was one where he pulled out every trick imaginable, right down to staffing trolls to work as a terrifying elevator in the center of the ride.

When Roman had announced it, the community had mocked and derided the idea of theming a star attraction to a troll attack. And perhaps that's why he took so many risks and employed so much magic, simply to drive home his point.

She shivered as she crossed into the glacier room. A barren white wasteland cold enough to make a polar bear feel at home. Instead, only the frozen body of a troll stood out in that place. Just below the surface, you could see the black eyes and shriveled skin of the giant. Thankfully, it was one of the ride's props and not an actual dead, 20-foot troll.

Or so she hoped.

The path led her behind an angled crevasse, hiding her from the boats as the narration built a terrible, foreboding mood. "For, you see, adventurers, it was not only the explorers who were lost to the wastelands."

Ellie crossed through a short hallway, black as pitch outside the distant ambient light.

It brought her to the center of the ride, where a towering animatronic troll, who was anything but, plucked one boat after another from the lower flume and moved it to an angled ramp some 15 feet above.

Thrud had eyesight that could make an owl jealous, and as one boat left her grip on the ramp, and before the next entered the room, her towering form winked at Ellie, gray fur bunching up around her eyes.

Ellie waved back and continued on, still amazed by the being's resilience in the cold with wet fur. Thrud said it was still warmer than her home in Iceland and had also informed her she didn't have to wear pants at home.

Maybe HR wasn't so bad.

With a small laugh, Ellie moved on from the sprawling waterfalls and recorded roars of a giant troll.

The next hallway cut off several scenes of the ride, but the path still took her through the final scene. The culmination of an odd story, where the riders went from hunting an angry troll to realizing a thief had stolen the troll's horde, and without it, their family would starve when summer arrived.

It reminded her of the tales of a dragon horde, but kinder. The last scene showed the spoils of the riders' new partnership with the troll, and a huge sprawl of treasure.

Gold and silver peeked from a stack of heavy, banded chests in a cave adorned with paintings that spoke to a side of trolls few would have considered. A home, welcoming travelers.

And at the center of that room, below the shelf that supported the boats and treasure alike, stood the giant bust of a much less angry troll. A kind expression on their face, and one of the most impressive animatronics Ellie had ever seen.

Riders gawked at the titanic head, many of them pointing and smiling and most often speechless.

Franzi, a slibreg who worked at the park, had told her about an early version of the ride they'd tested with screens and illusions that required the riders to wear 3D glasses. Apparently, the experience had annoyed Roman so much he immediately requested the design and build of the new head.

Ellie slipped behind one of the towering treasure chests and moved past a satin-like curtain. The noise cut off instantly, along with the golden glow reflected from the horde of treasure.

Unlike another park she'd once toured backstage, there were no harsh fluorescents in the hidden places, places where space felt longer and wider than it should have been.

Here, flickering torches and sconces lit the way. A place of calm between the literal storms of the dark ride. She almost didn't want to leave the vinegar halls, a nickname given to the place for the light scent that permeated everything in it. But as fast as the thought entered her mind, the load station came into view.

Most of the ride operators could have passed as human. A few could have passed as humans in light makeup.

The sapphire blue will-o'-the-wisps lighting the entrance tunnel to the ride could pass as neither. None of the humans who visited the ride suspected a thing, noting their presence as one of many special effects.

The Fae who visited, however, were terrified of them.

Ellie smiled and waved her hand in greeting when a wisp flashed like a bright blue flame. And then she was away from the intricately carved timbers of the inner queue line, meandering down a winding stone path that took her to the nearest walkway.

The dark ride was nearly halfway around the circle of the park from HR, so either direction meant she had the same walk to meet Gus.

Ellie chose the path of steam and brass and copper. Lost Empire was a sprawling land filled with some of her favorite scenery, from the smooth concrete made to look like rough, multicolored cobblestones to the towering stone wall that surrounded the mountain city façade.

Enormous pipes and lifts whined and buzzed all around while ancient cars puttered along a winding track at Puffing Demons. Airships, nearby, remained one of her favorites, even if it was the slowest ride in the park, and despite its remarkably uncreative name. The view was unparalleled.

She resisted the urge to stop and talk with some more of the ride ops and continued past the city façade and into a dystopian ruin of the same land.

There was something calm in the quiet of the ruins. Aged steel beams stretched to the sky, surrounded by the remains of old brick and gargoyles from a different time, or perhaps a different world.

The music soothed the weary parkgoers, and the simple refreshments were hard to beat. Ellie found it to be an amazing counter to Tinker's Escape, waiting to throw its riders over broken tracks and hurl them through violent, yet somehow smooth, elements.

Ellie crossed through the decaying arch that marked the end of the Lost Empire and continued into Town Square, a popular place to meet the park's anime mascots.

In the distance she could see Merrows Lagoon, a land filled mostly with water rides waiting to shower all ages in questionably blue water. But the characters at hand were some of her favorites in all the park.

Roman hadn't made a show or commercial out of the rotund, adorable, wide-eyed furballs yet, but Ellie wondered if it was just a matter of time. The meet and greets rotated, never having more than two of the characters out at once, likely due to the extra staffing required to have more, and their current shortage.

Each of the mascots represented one of the park's lands, dressed in denim and many-pocketed vests for the Dark Forest, goggles, leather, and gear-laden arms for Lost Empire, heavy furred coats for Howling Mountain, oversized snorkels for Merrows Lagoon, and the list went on. The one thing that stayed consistent was the cuteness overload.

She smiled when two kids squealed as their turn came around to take photos with the characters. Ellie turned her focus back to the path, finding a long line across the lake in the central hub that said Titania's Table must be packed for lunch.

A bridge took her over one of the streams that connected the lakes, where an archway carved from massive trees declared the next land the Dark Forest. It wasn't as wooded as one might expect from a land with that name, but it certainly had a lot of trees.

The rise and fall of a fiddle accompanied by the chords of an old guitar filled the air, telling Ellie one of the stage shows was in progress. The usual music in the area was darker, heavier, and quite good at being just a bit unsettling.

A skull peered over the path, peeking between the trees as she wandered by the long walkway that would take guests to the Mine. It might be a great dark ride, but the standout attraction for the land was still Gowrow's Cave.

The dark brown and green tracks of the outside section of the roller coaster wove through the forest, its iconic cobra roll the only part of the course left in plain sight. Ellie loved the basso rumble of the coaster and the screams that accompanied it.

She passed the entrance to the ride and slipped backstage into an employee-only area. It might not be themed as nicely as the sections of the park meant for the guests, but it was far from neglected. The path curved and twisted back until the cabin façade of HR and the office buildings beyond came into view.

Ellie headed for the front door, heavy oak framed by an arch of smooth stones, and stepped inside.

Chapter 3

INSIDE THE OFFICE, the illusion of a rural building evaporated. Cubicles and neat desks waited there, the long reception table empty but for an inbox and stack of manilla folders. The rapid hum of conversation and clack of a mechanical keyboard told her Gus was nearby.

It could have been any office in the world, before she turned the corner.

Gus looked up from his keyboard and held a finger up, his claws blurring across the keys. The squirrel-like Fae pulled off his headphones and leaned forward, clicking his teeth together before moving the mouse and spinning to face Ellie.

"Let me guess. Brownies?"

"Yes."

Capy, the resident guest relations expert and bearer of endless patience, slowly raised an eyebrow from her desk on the left. "Gus would be thrilled to discuss that." She bared her teeth in a smile, nose twitching.

"It's in their contracts! The occasional double shift is paid overtime."

That might be true, as even Ellie's contract had an overtime clause, but that wasn't the complaint. "They're working *triples*."

Gus gestured for her to sit down in the regular office chair beside his desk. His own elevated stools with backs on them weren't designed for humans. He wasn't as small as an actual squirrel, being larger than a brownie, but he was still quite petite.

Capy, on the other hand, loomed over Ellie when she stood, dragging her chair closer. Ellie had only recently learned that Capy's nickname came from the animal she most resembled, a capybara. As soon as Cole had mentioned that, Ellie was somewhat annoyed she hadn't realized the obviousness of it.

"Triples." Gus shuffled through several folders before pulling out a single piece of paper. "They aren't humans, you know? A triple shift every now and then won't kill them." He spun the paper around and flattened it on the desktop. "This is our standard agreement. Roman didn't even include any old-world tricks in it! Do you understand how unusual that is?"

Ellie squinted at the document. It was only one page, front and back, but the type was so small she doubted anyone could read it without a magnifying glass.

Gus ran his paw down it, searching, before tapping the page. "Here. 'Shortages and extraordinary circumstances may result in required overtime.'"

Ellie grimaced at him. "That's vague. What happened to no old-world tricks?"

Capy let out a low, barking laugh. "Perhaps that is something we could update, Gus? To help resolve our employees' misery?"

"Change the contract! We don't ..." Gus pinched the fur between his eyes.

The paper shifted when Capy pulled it closer. "Don't forget Roman's words, Gus. This is not Faerie."

"And no one should live in fear or hunger." The squirrel

sighed and flopped back in his chair. "I guess this *was* written a decade ago. We could update a few things. Make some amendments to the existing contracts? Things we understand better about this world after ten years."

Capy offered Gus a small smile before turning her gleaming teeth on Ellie. "See now, I will tell Bex and the others it's in the works and there's no need for more honey."

"That's great." Ellie rubbed her hands together. "But the root of the problem is Roman keeps approving too many vacations at once."

Gus threw his paws up in the air. "Do you know how many times I've asked him to double-check the schedule? Every time he just goes into the system and hits Approve All because it's *convenient*. Does he do that with the invoices? Noooo. But vacation time …"

"Perhaps you should consider Wendy's idea about hiring a developer?" Capy asked in her calm, placating tone. "I am certain the code could be updated."

Gus crossed his arms, eyes darting across the paper in front of them. "I'll talk to Roman about it. It might be the easiest fix to this. Getting Roman to change his habits. Well, you know."

Ellie's phone dinged. She unlocked it to make sure it wasn't any kind of emergency.

Cole: *Lunch?*

Ellie: *Yes*

Cole: *At café. Livestream in five!*

That couldn't be right. The livestream wasn't supposed to be until noon and … Ellie glanced at the time. *That damn churro.* "I have to go. You'll fix this, right, Gus?"

He sighed and gestured to Capy. "I'll work with her on it, Ellie. Go on. Enjoy the livestream."

She hesitated.

"He reads very well upside down," Capy said. "You will also find another sheet cake for no one's birthday."

Ellie blinked at that. "Because Gus 'forgot' again?" She gave the squirrel a sly glance.

He busied himself on his computer, not acknowledging the words.

Capy smiled. "Yes. Amazing how he can retain so much information except when it comes to birthdays. Almost as if he just wants more cake, isn't it?"

Gus narrowed his eyes but didn't rise to the bait.

"Wendy is out for part of this week, so you'll probably see a few more cakes in the cafeteria."

"Thank you both, really." Ellie stood and excused herself.

The employee café wasn't far, just out the door to HR and one building west. If she hurried, she could grab a tray and make it to the table in time. She knew Cole would already have the livestream up and waiting, and it always started a few minutes late, in case there were stragglers.

Her pace increased, hurrying to the tallest buildings at the back of the park. These were some of the only structures that wouldn't have looked out of place downtown. Of course, they'd been painted in a way they virtually disappeared against the sky. And it didn't much matter what the weather was like, the buildings just never caught anyone's eye. Another trick of the Fae, she suspected, though Roman would never admit to it.

Ellie barged through the front door, pushing her way inside, before a deep voice snapped at her.

"Watch it, girl!"

She nearly hopped back on instinct when she saw Bruce, the park's most notoriously grumpy security guard. "Sorry, I didn't see you there!"

"Always in a rush, aren't you? Give people their space, will you? Almost dropped my cantaloupe."

"Sorry, Bruce, really. I'm running a little late."

He gave her a curt nod and waited for her to step to the side.

She bristled but slid to the left. Sometimes it was easier to let the cantankerous wall of a man just walk away. If she'd had more time, she might have confronted him until he turned a concerning shade of red, but there were livestreams to be watched.

Bruce doubled as the food and health inspector as well, which was a pretty niche job when you considered all the Fae chefs in the park. She glanced back as he turned sideways to exit through the door, close-cropped salt and pepper hair almost brushing the door frame.

Confrontation avoided, Ellie rushed down the bright hall to the open doors of the café. It wasn't grand, exactly, a bit sterile, like her old high school cafeteria, but the food was always good. And free.

She grabbed a tray and dropped it on the silver rails in front of the counter. Chafing dishes hid whatever waited inside. Ellie slid the first open and found a pile of churros. While she'd normally jump at the chance to have a churro for an appetizer, or a snack, or an entire lunch, for some reason she wasn't feeling it.

The next dish held a teetering stack of burritos. Now *those* she could stomach. Ellie grabbed two and continued down the line, picking up a basket of fries from the warmer and a glass of water. She hesitated at the cake, then slid a respectable slice onto her plate. The name had already been sliced away from the white icing.

A quick look around the room showed her enough seats and tables to host at least a hundred employees, but only a handful had been filled. She picked Cole out and headed toward him.

He nodded and took a huge bite of churro.

Ellie pondered telling him about her churro experience that morning, but figured she'd let him work through things himself. Maybe Roman had already changed the recipe. She slid into the seat next to him, and while it looked like a hard plastic abomination one might find in any school cafeteria, it felt remarkably comfortable.

"Just in time!" Cole wiped his fingers off and pushed the volume up on his phone.

"Thanks for the reminder." Ellie unwrapped the foil around her burrito and bit in. A perfect tortilla, soft eggs, black beans, and rich salsa with just the right amount of heat. The fact nothing had gotten soggy was magic in itself.

Soon the countdown ended on the screen and the logo for *Taters' Rides and Guides* zoomed into view, a pair of russet potatoes riding over a roller coaster top hat. The screen resolved into a frame of Tottie waving, blonde space buns wobbling on top of her head, the soaring arches of the entryway framing her.

"We're back at the Theme Park at the End of the World!"

"And we still don't have a nickname for it," Poe muttered

from behind the camera. "What is it with parks and names? If it's not the name of the park, it's the name of the ride."

"Ignore my husband, folks. He's grumpy because he lost the coin flip for today's stream. So, he'll be paying for our lunch at Titania's Table." Tottie shot a wicked grin at Poe.

The camera swept down and when it came back up, they were both in the frame. Poe had a single dimple in his dark brown cheeks, and a close-cropped flattop, while Tottie had matching dimples below her space buns.

"It's all rigged." The muscles in Poe's sharp jaw flexed. "Statistically speaking, it should be impossible to lose this much."

Tottie walked backward through the arches, Poe taking his place behind the camera again as the Boardwalk came into view.

"Wow, look at the line for the Wild Mouse." Cole pointed at the screen as if Ellie wasn't looking at the same image.

"That's crazy." Ellie had rarely seen it backed up into the extended queue, but it was likely keeping the pretzel stand busy. The circus tent rose behind it, flanked by half a dozen carnival games along the eastern path.

"Probably needs more cars on the track."

Tottie skipped ahead, stopping at the Balloon Darts booth. She pointed at some of the new prizes hanging across the ceiling as Poe caught up to her. "Are you seeing these?"

Ellie smacked Cole's upper arm and grinned at him. She knew he'd helped pick the prizes out last week. When the Fae were left to choose prizes, well, sometimes they got a little too weird for their human guests. That was fine, during Fae park hours, but trying to explain why any kid should be interested in winning a variety of honey at a theme park was another story.

Poe zoomed in on the new prizes. "Potato plushies!"

"Potato plushies!" Tottie echoed. "I need one."

"Tottie."

"I *need* one."

"*Tottie.*"

The attendant smelled blood, stepping forward with a kind smile. "Five dollars for three darts. Pop three balloons and you have your pick of prizes, except for the potato."

"And for the potato?" Poe asked.

"Three balloons of the same color."

Poe swung the camera around and huddled in next to Tottie. "What do you think? It's not even the largest prize."

"Pfff, clearly, it's the highest *quality* prize, Poe. It's a potato!"

Poe didn't rise to the bait, but he still looked excited at the prospect of a plush potato.

The confused look on the attendant's face in the background made Ellie laugh.

"Think we can do it?" Poe asked.

"As long as you aren't throwing the darts."

Poe looked like he was about to argue, then shrugged, tilting the camera a hair with the motion. "You still can't beat me on the Mine."

Tottie shooed him away as he stepped out of the frame to continue filming. "Yes, yes, you and your shooter rides. Whereas *I* have useful hand eye coordination." She pulled her phone out and sidled up to the booth. "Three darts please."

She scanned her phone to pay when the attendant held out the reader. He laid out three darts, perfectly parallel to each other, which was the only real clue Ellie had seen that he wasn't human.

"When you're ready."

Tottie blew out a long breath.

"You got this, Tater Tot!"

She shot Poe a glare at the use of her supposed least-favorite nickname. But the glare cracked into a smile before she turned away and picked up the darts. Tottie didn't take much time to aim, hurling the first dart into a red balloon.

Cole hissed. "Bad choice. There are less of those on the board."

But the second dart found another red in the upper right corner, the balloon deflating with an explosive pop.

"One more!" Poe's excitement over the prospect of a stuffed potato was one of the reasons Ellie loved watching *Taters' Rides and Guides.*

She expected Tottie to wait and focus. She'd seen it play out dozens of times working the games, the guests getting nervous about the winning throw, which almost always led to a miss.

But Tottie didn't hesitate. She pulled her arm back and snapped it forward, dropping her wrist and following through with the release. The last balloon popped, and the attendant, without missing a beat, triggered the confetti cannons.

It was a little over the top, Ellie had to admit, but it was one of those things Roman had wanted. The laser lights were hard to see in the daytime, but the boom of the small confetti cannons was just as loud as the popping balloons.

"Go Tottie!" Poe shouted.

Tottie clapped her hands together and bounced on the balls of her feet.

"Congratulations! I'm guessing you want the potato?" The

attendant raised an eyebrow.

"Yes!" the Taters answered in unison.

With another congratulations from the attendant, they moved on, the giant looming pretzel of the pretzel booth flashing in the background before they exited Carnival and entered Howling Mountain. Bobsled, the park's wooden roller coaster, entered the frame as Tottie danced past the entrance, the sizable plush potato firmly planted on her shoulder.

"Your lunch is getting cold." Cole grinned when Ellie glanced up from the screen.

"Right, I should eat that."

Chapter 4

ELLIE FINISHED HER burritos while keeping one eye on the livestream.

"I didn't think the stream was going to be this long." Cole glanced at the time. "Half of our lunch is gone."

"Roman will understand," Ellie said. "He knows how much reach the Taters have. And … we're just adding to that reach!"

Cole raised a very skeptical eyebrow.

Ellie grinned and looked back at the screen.

The Taters had made it through Howling Mountain and into Lost Empire. They always skipped Tinker's Escape on the livestreams since they couldn't take a camera, but they did hop on Airships. And the views from the top reminded Ellie that she needed to get on that ride again.

Poe swept the camera from the mountains in Lost Empire to the Dark Forest, from Merrows Lagoon all the way to the entrance arches. While many parks had incredible theming, there was something about the Theme Park at the End of the World being nestled in the hills that made it feel *different*. It felt like home. Long before it had ever *been* home.

Ellie sighed and watched the banter between Tottie and Poe as they exited Lost Empire.

"The crowd levels are fantastic today," Poe said. "It's nice when the crowd calendars get it right."

"Just wait for the next event to start." Tottie cast a smile back at the camera. "You know those crowds are going to get wild again. We'll be seeing ninety-minute wait times on Tinker's Escape before you know it."

Poe groaned at the idea.

"The mascots are out!" Tottie said. "I need photos."

"Of course, because we've never done that before," Poe said. "What about lunch?"

"Priorities, Poe! Priorities." She grabbed his arm, so it looked like she had a hold of the camera, dragging both Poe and the audience along with her. "This is the first time we've been to the park since we moved into town!"

Ellie slapped Cole's forearm. "They finished their move! And they're heading this way through the park. I'm going to find them."

"Stalker."

Ellie hesitated. "I prefer 'very rabid fan,' thank you very much." With that, she slid out of her seat and dumped the last bits of food from her tray into the trash—excited noises rising from its depths—as she headed for the door.

The path she'd followed to reach HR and the cafeteria might have been a bit shorter, but the crowds always made it take longer than expected. She took the southern walkway to cut between Dark Forest and Merrows Lagoon.

Kraken's Fury loomed on her right, a tiered building of mountains with plateaus of grasslands and the water flumes for the ride weaving in and out at each level. Ellie shivered at the shadows above the entrance, as if unseen eyes tracked her steps. Merrows Lagoon was the most unsettling land in the park, in her opinion, though she knew a lot of folks gave that award to

Dark Forest.

The path swung north, taking her back onto the walkway by the central hub, and a quick walk to the mascots. She hurried around the bend, dodging a family with a plush unicorn they must have won from the crane games by the theater.

Ellie spotted Tottie and Poe snapping photos with the mascots. She scanned her badge at the rear gates and slipped in past the longest line, waving when she caught Tottie's eye.

She grinned when Tottie started her way. She loved feeding the Taters inside information about the park, and she knew they appreciated it too.

"Hi!" Tottie didn't lose a moment, handing off the dialogue to Poe as the mascots started to leave for break. She hurried over to Ellie. "How are you?"

"I'm great!" Ellie beamed. "We've been watching the livestream in the breakroom, so I thought I'd come say hi."

"I'm so glad you did. We have to wrap up this segment, but would you like to grab lunch? We have reservations for three at Titania's Table, but our third abandoned us for *responsibilities*."

"Yes, I'd love to." It didn't take two seconds for Ellie to answer, though in the back of her mind she was remembering how full she was from her first lunch, and how short on time.

"Great, meet us there in fifteen minutes. It's great to see you again."

Ellie nodded and then froze as Tottie walked away. She didn't have nearly enough time left on her lunch to go to another lunch and get back to her shift. There was a shot, though, if Roman was in a good mood.

She unlocked her phone and started typing.

Ellie: *Can I combine my afternoon breaks with lunch today*

Roman: *For what reason?*

Ellie: *Promoting the park with some vloggers*

Roman: *You may not combine your breaks today, but you may escort them and I will purchase their lunch. Provided they show us in a positive light.*

Ellie: *Done!*

Roman: *I will need you to cover half a shift on the Mine late this afternoon.*

Ellie: *Not a problem*

She wasn't entirely sure it was legal to ask for positive press, so she'd forget to mention that part. Besides, the Taters loved the park. It wasn't like they were going to say anything terrible. And Roman's response was better than she could have hoped. The second half of the shift could be grueling, as everyone got out of work and came to the parks, and those breaks were needed. Especially for mere mortals.

Ellie grinned and slid her phone into her pocket.

"Ellie." Someone hissed.

She turned to look for the voice but didn't see anyone there until a white-striped paw caught her attention. "Hans? What are you doing here?"

Hans gestured for her to come closer, his long, sloped nose twitching and vibrating the whiskers on his furry black face. "Can you help with the mascot's uniform? Iron was used in the manufacturing of the new Lost Empire costume." He held his hand up to show a healthy scar of recently singed flesh.

"Hans, are you okay? Of course I can help!"

"Fine, I'll be fine."

He pushed the door open a little wider, and she slipped into the dressing room. Beyond waited a roomful of pooka, which were utterly adorable creatures provided you didn't know anything else about them. Wide, round eyes, and soft fur that could be blown out until they almost looked like puffballs stacked on top of one another. Roman had given them sanctuary in return for not bringing doom on the human guests.

That … usually went to plan.

But they were tricksters and had the energy of children who had just devoured giant pixie sticks. They were also the models for the park's mascots, which meant the mascots were essentially pooka wearing pooka costumes. They rarely spoke, unless it was to deliver some great or terrible prophecy. Or once to tell Hans the sharp cheddar he'd hidden from Franzi had gone rancid.

All in all, they were perfect for the mascots.

Ellie crouched down by the pooka in question, his round black eyes watching her as she checked over the costume. "Are pookas hurt by iron?"

The pooka slowly shook his head from side to side, rabbit-like nose twitching.

"Good. Hans, pass me my old cosplay repair toolbox, would you?"

Hans rooted through a cabinet in the corner before retrieving a box that could have been mistaken for a first aid kit, if not for the lettering in black electrical tape that spelled Cosplay Medic. Among the assortment of glues, tapes, buttons, pins, thread, and a dozen over things essential to any emergency repair, Ellie had stashed a few heavy-duty zipper pulls.

She grabbed pliers and immediately tore the iron pull off

the pooka's costume before snapping the brass pull in place. It might have had trace amounts of iron in it, but not enough to hurt the most sensitive Fae in the parks.

The pooka huffed and nodded at her, his rabbit-like ears popping up straight for a moment before flattening back down so he could don his mascot head, which looked remarkably like his own head, minus the ears. He gestured to the zipper with one paw.

"Should be safe for Hans now," Ellie said. "Don't touch the teeth, though."

"Good advice for many situations." Hans stepped closer, his furry tail snapping back and forth a bit. He grabbed the brass pull and zipped the pooka up, all the natural orange fur hidden inside a decidedly unnatural orange costume. Hans rubbed his claws together and smiled at Ellie.

"Thank you."

The pooka jumped up to his feet and gave two spins as he threw his arms out to the side. Before Ellie could register what was happening, the mascot picked her up and carried her through the front curtain before letting her go with a squeak.

He waved to her, adjusted his tool belt, and waited for the next round of guests to come up for their photos. The attendant shuffled her off to the side, whispered an exhausted thank you, and then turned back to the crowd at hand.

Just another day at the Theme Park at the End of the World.

Chapter 5

ELLIE SIGHED AS she caught sight of Poe and Tottie waiting outside Titania's Table. Either their table wasn't ready, or they'd been waiting for her. That worked well either way. The pair studied the exterior, taking photos of the old whiskey barrels, the aged brick that had been imported from Ireland, and the lamps along the crenelations above.

She could just hear Tottie. "I'm telling you, that's a perfect shot for the B roll. It'll look great."

"Good news!" Ellie called out as she approached the pair. "The owner said lunch is on him, for all of us."

Poe blinked.

Tottie lit up. "The owner knows who we are?"

Ellie thought about explaining just *how* big of a fan she was and how she sometimes rambled to Roman longer than one of their vlogs would take to watch. Instead, she only said, "Yes."

Tottie turned to Poe. "You're still acting like you had to pay on camera. The public must see you lose the coin flip."

"I always lose the coin flip." Poe sighed. "At least I won't *actually* have to pay for it this time."

"Taters, party of three," the host called out.

"That's us!" Tottie dragged the trio to the gated entrance where the shadowy metal swung inward with no visible assistance.

The aged wood and dark stain of the interior greeted them like a long-forgotten pub in some ancient country. Exposed brick flanked the towering mantel of a fireplace on the far wall, the screen embedded with dozens of coats of arms, several with no human lineage.

Old photos framed by small spotlights helped give the illusion all the light in that place was coming from the candles and lanterns. The host took them past leather booths, both stamped and riveted with symbols from Faerie. To the average human, they'd look like little more than intricate Celtic knots. To the Fae who visited, they were reminders of home, and to some, a bittersweet one at that.

The host gestured to a large booth near the corner, a long semicircle usually reserved for larger parties. Poe slid in first, followed by Tottie and Ellie. Only once they were settled did the host pass menus out.

"Your server will be with you shortly."

Ellie slid the soft leather cover of the menu closer, glancing at the logo for Titania's Table before flipping to the first page. They changed it regularly, but there were always a few staples that remained. She'd seen reviews before that called the restaurant directionless and an abstract mess. But those critics didn't understand what Titania's Table was.

Every Fae, no matter where they were from, just like every human who dined there, could find something to remind them of home. Regional dishes from across the world, only sometimes with a little extra magic tossed in.

"Did you see the whiskey menu?" Poe asked. "It's as long as the rest of the menu."

"Longer. Would you like to see the rest?"

Ellie looked up when the newcomer spoke and grinned at who she found. "Ana!"

"Welcome back, Ellie. And these must be the Taters. Roman informed us we'd have guests for lunch. Please, anything you'd like to try, it's on the house."

Poe raised an eyebrow.

"Yes, even the whiskey. Though if I'm being honest, you can get that any day of the week. The Irish coffee today, well, that has a bit more magic in it. Just for flavor." She winked at Ellie when the others looked down at their menus again.

"Appetizers to start?"

"What do you recommend?" Tottie asked. "We've only been here a couple times and we always get the Reuben bites."

Ellie immediately wanted an order of Rueben bites. Gooey, cheesy, packed with corned beef, sauerkraut, and a stunning dipping sauce.

"One of my favorites!" Ana flashed a brilliant smile. "If you don't mind some heat, I'd recommend the goat curry."

"My favorite words," Tottie said. "We'll take an order of goat curry to start. Have any good Irish beers that aren't Guinness?"

"Guinness Blonde?" Ana chuckled at her own words. "Joking. It's more popular this side of the pond, but Smithwick's is excellent."

"I'll try that."

"And for your whiskey?" Ana asked, turning to Poe.

"I don't know."

"Try the Redbreast 27-year. Trust me."

"Okay." Poe glanced down at his menu and his eyes bulged. "Wait, that's crazy expensive."

"On the house. I'll be right back with that. Mexican Coke, Ellie?"

"Yes, please! I have to work tonight."

"You also have to get older before you try the good stuff." Ana shot her a grin and walked away.

Poe looked over at Ellie. "Thank you for this, really. We don't usually treat ourselves quite like this."

"You'll have to thank Roman. And not that you heard it from me, but I know he appreciates the extra exposure you bring to the parks. He's not the owner who goes out of his way to say thank you, though, so there's that."

Tottie gestured to the table and the surrounding restaurant. "Ellie, this is more than enough thanks. This is, I mean, we'd never spend that kind of money on whiskey. As much as Poe might like to."

"I'm so excited about this." Poe rapidly tapped his fingertips together.

"You don't mind if we take some footage of the food before we eat, do you, Ellie?"

"Of course not! As long as it doesn't get cold."

Poe sighed dramatically. "Truly, the cost of finding the best spot for a photo while walking around the park with fresh food. We've lost more than one churro to the icy depths."

"Poe, shut up." Tottie slapped his arm with a laugh. "Now, what are we getting for entrées?"

"More importantly, desserts!"

POE GESTURED TO the camera's screen. "See? I'm telling you, something is wrong with the sensor on this thing. It's like the image is stacked, but obviously it can't be. It's still on the camera!"

Ana shrugged. "It'll look fine for the vlog, Poe. Don't worry about it."

"Sometimes, I swear I'm losing my mind. Like the bubbles."

Ellie mimicked Ana's shrug. "It still looks good."

"And we got a lot of comments on your crazed rant about the bubbles, so kudos, Poe."

Poe glowered at them both.

Ellie felt more than a little relieved when he shut the camera off and stashed it on the bench. She knew exactly what had happened in that photo. One of the mascots hadn't been entirely hidden by their costume, and pookas never showed up on film. That created many aberrations, often dismissed as issues with film or drives or memory cards. But the bubbles were Fae too, at least those that didn't appear in photos.

Poe and Tottie knew a lot about the Theme Park at the End of the World, but Ellie wondered what they'd think if they knew the truth of the place. Part of her was sad they'd never find out.

Ana returned a short time later with a bowl of goat curry—decadent chunks of meat laden with sliced garlic, shreds of scotch bonnets in a slaw, and a rich green sauce. The smell alone was enough to make Ellie's mouth water, which meant she was probably going to make herself miserable by the end of the meal.

At least working the Mine later would offer some decent exercise.

The bartender followed with a tray of drinks. A Glencairn glass—the name for which had been drilled into her head over many months of sitting at the bar drinking milkshakes—for Poe, a perfect pour of Smithwick's for Tottie, and a Mexican Coke in a glass bottle for Ellie, wisps of carbonation still rising from the recent opening.

"Thanks, Liam!" Ellie said, beaming.

"Of course, my dear." His thick Irish accent was on full display. "Poe, I recommend you breathe slow and deep, nose to glass, before tasting. Savor it. Look for the subtlest notes on the first sip. And that's the last of the bottle, so there might be a little extra in your glass."

"Thank you, truly."

Liam inclined his head. "I leave you in Ana's capable hands."

"Next course?" Ana asked.

Poe was already snapping photos and taking slow, sweeping videos of the curry and whiskey.

"I'd like to try the beef and Guiness stew." Tottie tapped the menu.

"Excellent choice. Ellie? Meatloaf sandwich?"

She took a sip of her soda and grinned. "Yes, please."

Ana turned her attention to Poe. "And for you?"

He hesitated. "I heard you have a pizza pretzel that's not always on the menu."

"Oh?"

"With anchovies?"

Ana smiled. "That's not something we normally have here; it's more reserved for private events. I believe we can find one for you, though."

"Please don't," Tottie muttered.

Ana offered her a sympathetic smile. "For dessert, the chef

would like to prepare cloudberry cream over oatcakes. It's a favorite of our local trolls."

Tottie groaned. "I'm just glad your trolls don't live in our comment section. That sounds lovely."

"Excellent. Please enjoy."

Ellie had to choke back a laugh of surprise at Ana's mention of the trolls. Thrud and Yngvarr did love cloudberry cream and oatcakes. When they weren't working on Treasure of Troll Peaks, it wasn't unusual to find them in the warehouse-sized breakroom snacking on various Norwegian fare.

Poe ladled out the goat curry in three equal portions before passing the bowls around the table. He eyed the whiskey, took a deep breath, and finally tasted it. Then he sank into the booth and sighed. "Oh, wow."

"Good?" Tottie asked.

"You'll have to try this."

"I will, but *you* need to try the curry before it gets cold."

Ellie grinned at them both before pulling off shreds of meat and spooning up the rich broth. Some days it was better than others, but it was always excellent. Today was no different, the thyme and garlic blooming across her tongue before the heat and salt elevated the bite. The goat was tender, but chewier than some might expect. The texture was perfection next to the crisp slaw and herbaceous broth.

Poe cursed and closed his eyes. "I don't know what I was expecting, but it wasn't that. I could eat an entire meal of this stuff!"

Tottie sighed and nodded in agreement.

Ellie finished her bowl before taking another sip of Coke. It was her favorite version of the drink she'd ever tried, cane sugar making all the difference. She smiled at Tottie and Poe as they indulged in their own drinks. Ellie still couldn't quite believe she was spending so much time with the Taters.

It felt like home in that moment, there at Titania's Table.

Chapter 6

THEY MADE IT through the beef and Guiness stew, meatloaf sandwich, and almost all of Poe's pretzel. Well, most of the way. Ellie stopped halfway through her sandwich and donated it to the Taters. Poe loved the pretzel, and Ellie was somewhat curious how he'd heard about it. Clearly some of the Fae talked a little too openly about the after-hours food.

Of course, Ellie was sometimes the Taters' anonymous source for inside information, so she didn't have much room to talk, either. She eyed the last bite of pretzel as Poe finished it.

The anchovy-stuffed pretzel was one of Capy's favorites, though Ellie always found it a little too salty. Well, a *lot* too salty. Apparently, Poe loved the flavor combination with his whiskey, but Ellie couldn't imagine how anyone could taste much of anything after biting into that pretzel.

Tottie leaned over conspiratorially. "So, any word on the spring event yet? Any chances of a Mardi Gras this year? We *need* it."

"Still no Mardi Gras." Ellie didn't quite manage to keep the disappointment from her voice. "But this summer we're getting Corn Dog Crave Days."

"We're getting what?" Poe leaned back and raised an eyebrow. "That's the name?"

Ellie grinned. "Yep, apparently going to be the official

name."

"I'm not mad about it." Tottie gestured to Poe. "We love corn dogs. But put a word in to the boss about doing Mardi Gras one year. Some of the other parks do an amazing job with it."

"I will. I know Roman spent some time in New Orleans, so it might be something he'd like to do."

Ana swung by the table one last time, handing out three beautifully arranged plates. A large oatcake, which didn't look much different from an oatmeal cookie, sat in the center, piled with three quenelles of fresh whipped cream and a cluster of sugared cloudberries. They reminded Ellie of raspberries, but a bit more orange.

"This is beautiful." Tottie slid her plate a little closer. "Please tell the chef thank you."

"I will. I hope you've enjoyed your meal at Titania's Table today. If you wish to leave an offering, you'll find her tree in the courtyard out back."

And *that* was likely why many Fae avoided the restaurant. Theme park or not, most of the Fae guests were afraid Titania herself might one day make an appearance regardless of an offering, or the lack of one. And not even the Fae were entirely sure of the ancient queen's machinations.

Poe went to work with his camera again, but Tottie didn't wait.

"I don't want this to melt."

Ellie broke the edge of the oatcake with her spoon, scooping up some cream and berries with it before shoveling the huge bite into her mouth. There was a quick burst of butter from the oatcake, almost like shortbread, before the whipped cream overtook it. The cloudberries burst, tart with a hint of sweetness made stronger by the sugar.

"What. The heck." Tottie's spoon clinked against her bowl. "This is amazing! It's just berries and cream, but it's amazing."

Poe sat his camera down and dug in, nodding along with everything Tottie had to say. "It beats my mom's oatmeal cookies, that's for sure. Probably shouldn't say that on camera, though."

They finished the dessert in silence until there was little left but a smear of cream on the simple dishes.

Ellie leaned back in the booth and blew out a breath. "I'm stuffed."

"I could eat more," Poe said, but he was betrayed by the slight groan in his words.

Tottie chuckled at that. "You could always eat more. But that was perfect."

"I have to head over to the Mine for a shift," Ellie said. "You two are welcome to stay and order more if you want."

"No way." Poe shook his head. "We've taken enough in hospitality from the park. Besides, I need to start editing. We filmed three episodes today."

"Three?" Ellie asked. "While you were doing the livestream?"

"Before." Tottie sipped the last of her Smithwick's. "We need a little more B roll of the park on the way out."

Poe sat up straighter. "And an intro. We didn't record an intro for the third video."

"Well, it's going to be about the restaurant, so why don't we film it out front before we go? It'll take ten minutes, at most."

"Good idea."

Tottie turned to Ellie. "Thank you, again. You're the best insider we could ask for."

Ellie didn't quite stop the grin that lifted the corners of her mouth. "You know how to reach me. Let me know if you have questions and I'll see if I can help. And anytime you all want to meet up, I'll be there."

"Thanks, Ellie." Poe stood and stretched his back, Tottie following.

She eyed Ellie. "Are you a hugger?"

"Yes!"

Tottie smiled and wrapped her up in a quick hug. Poe did the same, though it was one of those awkward half shoulder one leg out things he often did with the characters in the parks. Great for photos, a little weird for goodbyes.

"Oh, and Poe?" Ellie said.

He raised an eyebrow.

"If you ever want to be destroyed on the Mine, I'll ride with you."

Tottie snorted a laugh.

ONE SMALL THING Ellie loved about working at this park, in particular, was the costuming and changing rooms at every ride and venue. No lugging your uniforms through the park, or wearing them through the park, and switching attractions mid-shift was far easier when everything you needed would be waiting there.

It also meant she could go straight from a fantastic lunch to the Dark Forest, the path winding past Gowrow's Cave before she came to the Mine. Nothing else in the park was quite as intimidating as the massive, polished skull set into the towering face of the ride. The building was made to look like the cutaway side of a mountain, where the entrance had been framed by lumber just below the skull.

The employees entered through a small shack structure to the left of the façade, and that's where Ellie went. Darkness waited within, and it took a moment for her eyes to adjust before she traversed the short hallway to the better-lit changing rooms.

She grabbed a uniform in her size and ducked into one of the five empty stalls. The Mine had a simple, but layered outfit, designed to give riders the illusion that the attendants were guides in the hunt for rare cryptids. But it wasn't any hunt. It was a quest to save the endangered critters. Instead of rifles or lasers, they had tranquilizer guns, and the more cryptids you rescued, the more points you scored.

There were other targets, of course—poachers, and bears and various animals that wanted to eat everything you were trying to save. But the single thing Ellie heard the most was how responsive the props were. You could hold down the trigger and fire an intermittent burst that showed not only the color of your dart, but the shape of the icon you chose, too.

An announcement sounded over the loudspeaker. "Please remain seated. We are experiencing technical difficulties. The ride will resume momentarily."

Ellie hurried to fasten her belt and tie her shoelaces before tossing her supervisor's uniform in a locker. She wouldn't have any kind of authority while working the shift on the Mine. She was only a supervisor around the park when they needed her to be. When it was time to work in ride ops, whoever was shift lead was the effective supervisor.

That suited Ellie just fine. Roman didn't run the park in quite the same way as humans would have, so anyone working so much as a single hour as a supervisor received that pay rate, ongoing. She suspected that was to earn some good will among the Fae who worked there, but whatever the reason, she was just happy to have it.

Ellie hurried down the back hall, small lights along the baseboards showing the way to a hidden door. Inside, fans whirred, and intermittent clicks sounded as the air conditioning turned the server room into little more than a freezer.

Nessa's tall form sat hunched over a keyboard, glasses holding back her coily black hair as she muttered to herself in a language Ellie didn't know. For that matter, it was a language no mortal had heard in millennia, if the brownies were to be believed.

"Everything okay?" Ellie asked.

Nessa glanced up before rubbing the smooth, dark skin of her cheek. "Hey, Ellie. Almost. Just rebooting the relays for the sensors. Some of the targets weren't registering. Or everyone suddenly became terrible shots when the hinge-tailed bingbuffer popped out."

The name never failed to cause amusement. Ellie coughed to hide her laugh. "Need any help?"

Nessa slammed the Enter key and leaned back. "I don't think so. You're covering the afternoon shift, right?"

Ellie nodded.

"Good. You mind taking a ride through? Hit all the secret targets? I want to make sure everything's working again."

"No problem!" It was a rare thing to get a solo ride through the Mine, and Ellie would jump at any chance she could for that.

Nessa clicked through another series of menus to restart the ride. "All set. Go save some critters."

Ellie gave her what was likely the worst salute in history, judging by Nessa's perplexed expression. She headed back to the dark halls and followed them past the changing room. Nessa was the park's resident engineer. Some of the Fae weren't overly fond of electronics, preferring to rely on magic, but any time Roman said they were getting something new, Nessa lit up.

While Ellie wasn't sure how old Nessa actually was, a lot of technology was brand new in the eyes of the Fae. For some, it was a welcome change, coming from a world like Faerie that did not change at speed.

Another left took her to the loading station. The ride attendant spotted her immediately and pulled out one of the tranquilizers, handing it to Ellie and pointing to the next car.

"Solo ride! Enjoy."

Apparently, they already knew what Nessa wanted.

It made sense, Ellie supposed, as she slid into the six-seat trackless vehicle. Nessa knew how obsessed Ellie had been with maxing out her score as soon as the new ride opened. Calling it an obsession might have been an understatement.

Ellie grinned when the ride attendant lowered the padded lap bar and gave her the safety spiel.

"Do not run away from the bears. They're faster than you. Remain quietly seated at all times, unless you need to scream. And no flash photography, please. You'll scare the cryptids."

With that, the vehicle turned from the attendant and started forward into what at first appeared to be a deep forest before the path rounded a bend and opened on a replica of the exterior façade. Here, the skull was no mere polished icon. Grime and vegetation surrounded it, dark red LEDs lighting the depths of its sockets and casting shadows where its lower jaw should have been.

Most people didn't know there was a target hidden just below the teeth. Ellie took aim and pulled the trigger, the tranquilizer gun vibrating in her hand as the scoreboard jumped on the console.

The vocal track started, perfectly synced. "Get ready, team. If we're going to save these cryptids, we have to be fast. Get as many points as you can by keeping them safe." The sounds of a revving engine joined the birds and insects of the woods as the vehicle lurched forward.

Ellie set the butt of the tranquilizer gun against her shoulder and held the trigger down. It would only vibrate if she hit something, and that was key to figuring out how to aim. She swore no two units on that ride aimed the same way. Whoever had built them didn't pay much attention to making them shoot straight.

The first shaft of the mine was deceptively simple—the passage framed by rough timbers and the walls made to look like stone—but there were more targets than there appeared to be. Giant millipedes and more waited in the corners, barely visible but for the subtle glow of their targets. Ellie hit the first three, which opened a secret in the wall, the flickering shadow of something that looked a bit like a dinosaur waiting inside.

The stock vibrated in her hand when she hit it, and a quick glance at the display showed a massive bonus. Ellie focused on the right, watching for the next room as the hall narrowed briefly. Her reticle, a simple red X, swept across the space, casting the same image wherever she aimed.

Boulders shifted forward as a great roar filled her ears. A strange beast appeared, with skin like an elephant, but shaped more like a hippo. The hinge-tailed bingbuffer whipped a prehensile tail back and forth with a massive stone ready to throw. Ellie hit the target on the tail, causing it to drop, before taking aim at the front and rear legs.

The animatronic slowly lowered to the ground, thunderous snores accompanying the movement. A quick turn to the right showed the poachers' approaching floodlights from the opposite direction.

You couldn't hit them directly, as Roman thought some might consider that in poor taste, but you could aim for the tires. A boom like a blowout sounded, and the vehicle spun away with a jet of fog, back into the dark. It was almost more fun to miss the poachers, so your own vehicle would spin instead, but Ellie wanted to test the targets.

The next hall had a handful of bats. No hidden bonuses there, but the second to last room opened up around her, a waterfall projected in the distance, giving the illusion of a giant cavern.

That place was a watering hole, a gathering ground for some of the highest-point targets in the entire ride. The hardest to hit were the zigmals, squirrel-like creatures who propelled themselves through the air by bouncing on their tails. But if you knew where they landed, you could catch them.

One after another, each hit vibrated through Ellie's hands. Tracing the edge of the waterfall, she found another of the hidden targets, one that wouldn't be obvious until the next section of the ride. They turned toward the waterfall as the vehicle slowed.

The narrator cried out. "The road is crumbling! We have to get out of here!"

Ellie grinned as the vehicle shuddered from side to side, the sounds of gravel pinging against the doors, echoing up all around before huge cracks sounded. The roar of falling rock followed.

The entire track dropped beneath the vehicle, and Ellie shouted with joy in the free fall. She swooped forward at the bottom, bursting out of the far side of the mine past the waterfall and into another forest scene.

"That was close! Glad we made it. I think we're just about … get ready team!"

The last scene opened before her as a sunken den was revealed. Two scaly round balls popped their heads up, adorable creatures out of folklore known as gowrows. Of course, those wide eyes, and long snouts weren't nearly so adorable when they grew up, which guests could see in the Gowrow's Cave roller coaster. Ellie hit both targets, then swung to the left. On the opposite side of the room was a tiny view of another poacher's vehicle.

A precise shot through the leaves gave her the last bonus of the ride, and the tranquilizer dinged in her hand. The display showed 999,999. The most anyone could score.

"Well done, team. You'll make fantastic cryptid conservationists. Now, please keep your hands inside the vehicle until we come to a complete stop. Don't forget to adopt your own cryptid today in the visitor's center!"

The cast members applauded as Ellie's vehicle slowed to a stop in the station. She hopped out as the bar rose, handing her tranquilizer gun off to the attendant.

"Everything looks good! I'll let Nessa know. After I stop by the visitor's center, of course."

The ride ops laughed and waved as Ellie veered away from the exit and walked backstage. The hallways here were just as dark as those by the data center, but the lighting along the floor was much the same. She followed them to a short set of stairs that took her over the free fall and was used for evacuations in the rare case the ride malfunctioned.

It wasn't long before she opened the door to the server room and slipped inside.

"Well?" Nessa asked. "I didn't see anything wrong on this end."

"Everything worked great. I hit every bonus and most of the zigmals. All three of the major targets in the bingbuffer scene, too. Plus the poachers."

Nessa gestured to Ellie. "You're pretty good for a human. I'll give you that." She tapped a fingernail on the side of her keyboard. "We should be good, then. Would you mind taking a ride through once an hour for this shift? I want to make sure everything's ready for the Fae hours."

Ellie put her hand over her heart. "I suppose I can endure riding a few more times in my frail human body."

"Enough practice and you could max out the score one room earlier." Nessa smirked at her. "Get out of here before I put you on sanitation detail."

Ellie vanished almost the instant Nessa finished speaking.

THE REST OF the evening was rather uneventful, though hopping into empty seats once an hour to assist various families as they journeyed through the Mine helped the time pass. The youngest of them were usually Ellie's favorite, so taken in by the story and theming they literally believed they were there.

But that night was different. A vehicle packed with twenty-somethings dressed up in ridiculous safari shirts and hats was definitely the highlight. They were almost as excited for Ellie to be joining them as they were for the photo op in the middle of the ride.

Ellie had little doubt that was going to end up on a few social media sites. She smiled as she walked through the park, much quieter now as they prepared for a short shift of Fae hours. Weekdays weren't like the weekends, where the Fae hours constituted a full shift. That was partially due to noise ordinances, and partially due to the fact even Fae needed some time off.

A raised voice caught Ellie's attention as she walked through the Howling Mountain land toward her apartment. Unsurprisingly, she found Bruce trying to lecture one of the pooka.

"You can't wander the park without your costumes on a weekday! Not even after hours. How many times do I have to tell you? Is there a single active brain cell inside that furry melon of yours?"

Ellie waved at the pooka.

He responded with a slow blink.

She pointed toward the path beyond, gave him a deliberate nod, then shouted. "Hi, Bruce! How are you this evening?"

The security guard spun on her. "What are you doing out? I thought your shift ended this afternoon." His eyes narrowed.

"Nah, Roman asked me to take half a shift on the Mine." She didn't look him in the eye, as that always set him off, and kept a good distance from him. "Just heading off to get some sleep. Going to be a long one tomorrow, too." She continued walking until Bruce started to turn back around. "Say, Bruce, weren't you supposed to be off already, too? Seems late."

"I'm always watching, Ellie. Nothing gets through our security because of *me*."

Ellie flashed him a broad smile. "Have a good night, Bruce."

He spun away from her to continue his lecture of the pooka, but the pooka had taken Ellie's cue and long since vanished down the nearby path.

Bruce literally threw his hat on the ground.

Ellie bit her lips to avoid laughing and never looked back.

Chapter 7

AFTER A LONG afternoon shift, Ellie nested into her apartment. The small studio didn't look like much at first glance, but it had everything she needed. The soft rug with its oversized shag, a tiny fireplace in the corner with a wood stove and kettle. Although she rarely used the copper kettle, as the electric one was easier for a good cup of tea. For that matter, she used the toaster oven more than the stove.

The bed stood around the corner, flanked by floor-to-ceiling bookshelves, giving the apartment a sense of having more rooms than it did. With storage underneath the bedframe and extra in the bathroom, it was all the space she wanted.

One of her favorite things was that the apartments behind Howling Mountain were themed on the inside as much as the outside. The contrast of exposed wooden timbers and plaster with the latest anime posters and theme park souvenirs might have been jarring to most people, but to Ellie, it felt like home.

She pulled a fleece blanket tighter and leaned back into the overstuffed leather loveseat, switching off from her newest book to watch an episode of *Taters' Rides and Guides* before going to bed. It was one she'd already watched a few times, with the food review of Titania's Table and the mascots from the week before.

Ellie was drifting off when her phone dinged. She cracked

one eye open and frowned.

> **Roman:** *Teak is stuck. Please help at the rope climb.*
>
> **Ellie:** *Now?*
>
> **Roman:** *Yes. He is upside down.*

It was such a ridiculous response that Ellie just burst into laughter. That's what she got for unwittingly volunteering to be on Teak duty. She threw off her blanket and sighed, padding over to the heavy wooden wardrobe to grab a pair of jeans and a BABYMETAL T-shirt.

The rope climb wasn't too far from her apartment. The walk took her past the Bobsled coaster and down onto the Boardwalk, where the attraction waited behind a row of carnival games and the Whimsy Carousel.

During the day, it was a simple thing to traverse. Once the Fae hours started, the rope climb became something else. Towering four stories into the air, the tight surface sagged with deep valleys and hills that defied logic. It was one of the few Fae attractions Ellie could safely indulge in.

It was certainly more fun than a regular rope climb, but it wasn't unusual for some Fae to get themselves stuck. Especially Teak.

She found him on the second level, almost entirely upside down at the crest of a hill, owl-like talons splayed in the air and feathered wings limp in a show of utter defeat. Ellie wasn't sure why Teak insisted on working the rope climb. It rarely ended well once the ropes shifted into their slackened forms for the Fae hours.

"Hi, Ellie." Teak blinked at her with unmoving eyes, not quite able to shift his head in the tangle of ropes.

She stood back a bit in a deep valley of ropes, trying to figure out *how* she was going to untangle him this time. The usual Fae solution was to cut the ropes and bounce him down to the entrance, but after Ellie complained about that not being very nice, she'd been nominated official Teak wrangler.

"What did you *do*?"

"A pixie said they were stuck, so I flew over to help, but they weren't *actually* stuck. Another pixie had pulled the hill into a valley, and they let it go when I circled and—"

Ellie held her hands up. "Never mind, Teak." Pixies were mischievous on their best days. Put them in a theme park around other Fae and they were just as much trouble as the most troublesome human teenagers. Which Ellie always felt weird saying, being she was one.

Studying the tangle of rope a bit more, she could see the problem. Teak had likely grabbed hold of the ropes with his hands as he circled. Not *hands*, exactly, but Teak had remarkably posable wings and feathers that worked much like a human's hands. It wasn't enough to get him untangled, though.

"I think we need to twist you around a bit, then get that loop out from under your right leg." Ellie tapped her chin and squinted at the rope some more.

"My wing is stuck, too." He wiggled the feathers to show the level of stuckness.

Ellie sighed and leaned forward, grabbing the base of the rope hill and climbing it like a ladder. It didn't take more than a minute to reach the top, even moving slowly, but it left her perched somewhat precariously beside the owl.

She shuffled around to the back, making sure Teak hadn't managed to get his tail feathers in a knot either. That had happened last month, and she hadn't thought she'd ever hear the end of it when she gave up and cut the ropes herself.

Ellie grabbed the rope pinching Teak's wing and twisted, opening the gap a little wider. "See if you can get your wing out."

If he'd had more room to maneuver, it likely wouldn't have been an issue, but Ellie had to pull a little harder, forcing the ropes down with her foot as she lifted as hard as she could. Arms shaking, she was about to give up when Teak hooted.

"My wing's free!"

Ellie blew out a harsh breath and let the ropes spring back into their natural state. "Okay, give me your wings. We're going to turn to the right a bit."

Teak reached out, locking his wings against her arms as Ellie pulled, slowly twisting the first layer of knots apart. The owl dropped a few inches when the first tangles snapped into their normal positions, the sudden weight yanking Ellie forward.

"I can move my head." He turned and caught Ellie's gaze, large amber eyes locking on to hers. "Sorry about this. Again, I mean."

"It's okay, Teak. I just don't want them throwing you down to the entrance anymore."

"It was kind of fun the first time." His voice trailed off. "After that, not so much."

Ellie laughed and grabbed Teak's ankles, pushing him to the side until another tangle released. "Next one is going to snap with all the tension. You ready?"

Teak nodded as best he could.

A hard twist of the ropes did nothing. Ellie blew out her

breath and rested her head on the knot. "I'm going to need a hand with this one. Can you push down here?" She guided his bristly feathers to the rope she needed forced apart.

"Got it."

She nodded. "Okay, on three." Ellie counted down and then pushed to the left with everything she had.

The rope gave way with a twang, springing back into the floating hill, the release throwing Teak into the air where he somersaulted once, then landed lightly back on the ropes that had trapped him.

"Thanks, Ellie!"

She smiled at the owl. "No problem, Teak. Now, keep an eye out for those pixies next time."

Even before she finished speaking, the high-pitched laughter of those chaos makers filled her ears.

"I heard that!" She put her fists on her hips and scowled.

Streaks of sparkling light chased the laughter as the pixies zipped away, looking for their next target.

Ellie looked up at Teak. "You good for the night, Teak? I can see about getting you an extra break."

"I'm fine, Ellie. Just stuck. And now unstuck." His eyes squinted a bit in what Ellie had come to recognize as a smile.

"Okay, I'm going to get some sleep. I'll see you tomorrow!"

With that, she made her way back down the ropes, passing a group of slender Fae who looked utterly bored as they walked across the ropes, so light on their feet the mesh barely shifted. Other groups weren't nearly so unenthused.

A cluster of shretma kids, whiskers twitching on their furry, sloped faces and puffy cheeks, raced around the ropes in a game of tag. It reminded Ellie of line tag when she was younger. No diagonals allowed; each player had to follow the lines of whatever structure the game was played on. Even a parking lot would do in a pinch.

"No cheating, bro!"

Ellie turned to find Manfred, one of the shretma who managed the retail stands around the park. Much like the slibreg, they showed up on film so didn't need to wear a costume in the park. Instead, they pretended to be wearing a suit, and that … did not always go well. It didn't help that Manfred, along with Katinka, said bro so much, which annoyed Roman so badly he'd literally given them scripts to follow.

She waved to Manfred and his whiskers twitched.

"Teak stuck again?" he asked.

"Yep."

"Bro."

"I know. Have a good night, Manfred!"

A kid dropped through the ropes and scampered across the bottom, the others screaming *cheater* as he sprinted away upside down.

"Bro, no!" Manfred's attention went fully back to the game of tag. Apparently, he was the referee of that chaos.

Ellie continued down the rope climb, reaching the exit in short order before she saw someone she hadn't realized was back. "Hi, Wendy!" Ellie raised her hand in greeting as the sharply dressed elephant walked by.

Wendy greeted her with a wave of her trunk. "Hi, Ellie. I've been working on the schedule, making some of those changes for the new PTO system. Can you work a double tomorrow?"

Sometimes it was better not to say hi, Ellie reminded herself.

"It would help me out a lot," Wendy said.

"Of course!" As soon as she spoke, Ellie remembered tomorrow was Saturday. She almost banged her forehead on the entrance support when she realized what that meant. Lots more Fae kids on Saturday nights. Lots more chaos. Maybe one day Roman would get her one of the tattoos that would let her ride the Fae rides without, you know, *dying*. But sometimes it felt like dying was what it would take to get him to say yes.

"Ellie?" Wendy said tentatively. "Are you okay?"

"Yes, yes, I'm great. Where did you need me?"

"How would you feel about working Tinker's Escape?"

"During Fae hours? Really?" She couldn't quite keep the skeptical note out of her voice.

"Just don't try to ride it. Good human help is hard to find." Wendy trumpeted a laugh through her trunk and continued on.

"Hilarious," Ellie muttered.

Teak landed beside her, clicking his beak together and failing miserably to hide a laugh.

ELLIE TOOK THE long way out of Carnival, wandering down the wooden path of the Boardwalk until she arrived at the pretzel stand. She blinked when she recognized Cole at the back of the line. Instead of saying anything or announcing herself, she simply ran into him in a tackle hug.

"Oh, excuse me, I didn't see you there."

Cole laughed, and annoyingly didn't stumble a single step. "What are you still doing up?"

"Teak," she said through a sigh.

"Ah, yes. I thought I heard a familiar squawk in the distance."

Ellie slapped his arm and pulled away. "Getting an anchovy pretzel?"

Cole almost recoiled. "Look, the Taters might be crazy enough to like those, but I'll stick with pepperoni, thank you very much."

"Do they have them for Fae hours tonight?" Ellie perked up and stood on her tiptoes, trying to see the pretzel case. She caught sight of Franzi hurrying back and forth, filling orders as fast as they came in.

"Did you see the human, Mom? I didn't think they were really in the parks when we were here!"

Ellie looked around and found an adorable capybara Fae looking at her in awe. She smiled and waved.

The mom gave her a toothy smile before ushering the kid away, a frozen popsicle filled with pumpkin seeds and alfalfa hay clutched in their paw. Now *that* was a treat you wouldn't find at human theme parks.

There were times in the park when everything felt right with the world. Standing there with Cole as the world moved around them brought her a kind of peace she couldn't fully explain. Some company could fill you up like a rich tea. Or a pizza pretzel.

"Hey, Franzi," Cole said. "Do you have more of the pepperoni pretzels tonight?"

Franzi's furry tail whipped from side to side, and she scratched the white streak of fur running down her nose before washing her claws. "We do. Two?" She eyed Ellie.

On the one hand, Ellie didn't feel like she needed that much food for a snack. On the other … "Yes, please!"

Franzi tapped the touchscreen on the register. "I heard you rescued Teak again. On the house tonight."

"Thank you!" Ellie clapped her hands and grinned at Cole.

A moment later, Franzi handed over two thick, soft pretzels, coated in crusty toasted cheese, and filled with mozzarella, pepperoni, and marinara. Cole said his thanks, and they continued down the boardwalk, stepping off the wooden path and onto the decorative concrete that would take them past the Wild Mouse.

The coaster was aggressive during the day, but at night, when the ride shifted into a true Monster Mouse, it earned its name in full. The night ride soared twice the height of the normal coaster. Two launches sat in the middle of the track to ensure the ride vehicles didn't valley in the extra depths. The screams from Monster Mouse were nearly on par with the park's largest coasters.

Ellie bit into her pretzel as they wandered by the entrance queue, bright amber bulbs lit up like an old-world carnival. The burst of cheese and sauce and salt chased away all thoughts of the towering ride beside them. She crunched through the pepperoni, savoring the rich contrast of the meat with the brightness of the marinara.

"You can't beat these." Cole shook his pretzel at her.

Ellie took a bite, large enough to make the Taters proud. She hadn't quite chewed it up enough to talk, but that didn't stop her. "I'm not arguing."

Their path took them by the Whimsy Carousel, another Ellie could ride as a human, though it was a bit of a nightmare during the Fae hours. The warm and friendly animatronics sprang out like the scare actors in a haunted house and the normally solid floor rose and fell between three different levels beneath the tent.

She hadn't ridden it in a while and made a mental note to fix that soon.

"We need to do this more often again, Ellie." Cole flashed her a small smile.

"I know. We've been working too much. Maybe instead of a raise, Roman will give us more time off. That would be great, wouldn't it?"

"So great. I'd like to go see some more parks. You know, some of them aren't that far away? We could do a road trip. Stop at Wally's or Buc-EE's and get ridiculous snacks. I couldn't tell you the last time I was on a road trip."

She started to reach out to squeeze his arm, then remembered the sheer quantity of pizza pretzel grease on her hands. "I'd like that a lot, Cole. One of us probably needs to buy a car then."

He laughed at that. "Probably. Maybe we can borrow one. Or rent, if it's in the budget. Next summer?"

"Gives us a year to save up. Let's plan on it!"

Cole beamed at her.

"You going home for the night?" Ellie asked.

He nodded and drifted closer as they wandered out of Carnival. "Definitely. I don't have to work third shift, and my swing shift is done." He gestured to his *Totoro* T-shirt. "No more work today."

They walked in silence for a time, taking in the screams from the Bobsled in the distance and the rumble of Treasure of Troll Peaks. The sound deadened as they reached the apartments behind Howling Mountain.

Ellie finished her pretzel and wiped her fingers on a napkin as Cole did the same.

He stepped toward her before hesitating, then offering a smile. "Sleep good. If you're working a double, it's going to be a rough day."

Ellie groaned.

<h1 align="center">Chapter 8</h1>

ELLIE TOOK A deep breath as she stood in the locker room for Tinker's Escape. She'd never gotten to work ride ops there on a Fae night. Just *seeing* the transformation was exciting, but being able to work the load station with all the Fae coming in and out was going to be amazing.

It didn't matter how many times she'd been trained on something. The first time she tried it in practice, she couldn't shake her nerves. Ellie didn't want to let Kevin down, or the shift leads, or anyone else working ride ops with her.

She took another breath, held it for a moment, then blew it out, forcing herself to relax. Ellie knew everything about Tinker's Escape. She knew what changed from day to night, where the block zones were, what the evacuation points were, and she could practically walk the entire track blindfolded.

Ellie nodded to herself and started down the hall. It wasn't as dark backstage as the dark rides, especially the Mine, but the small strips of light on the ground still guided everyone to where they needed to be. It would be a long night, and she might as well have as much fun as she could before exhaustion set in.

The roar of the launch echoed through the tunnel as the lights of the station came into view. Her steps slowed when she saw a familiar face talking to Kevin at the end of the tunnel.

"Cole!"

They both looked down the tunnel and squinted.

"I didn't know you were working here tonight, too," Cole said. "Your first night on Tinker's Escape! Letting the humans out to play for a bit, I guess."

Kevin grinned. "Yes, we hear that's healthy for you human types." He tapped the tablet in his hand. "Cole, I want you on the queue side of the trains. Ellie, work the opposite. I want dispatch times short and restraints *very* secure. Staple them into those seats."

Ellie could just imagine the horror-stricken faces of coaster enthusiasts at Kevin's instructions. Stapling, where the lap bar was so tight you couldn't move much in the seat, could take a lot of fun out of a ride. One thing that was amazing about Tinker's Escape was that even stapled, it felt like the train was trying to throw you off the ride. And that was during *human* hours.

Kevin held both of their gazes. "You two have any trouble, any doubts, you call for me. There's a radio on either side at the front of the platform. Don't hop across the tracks. Use the walkway. You fall during the day, you might break a leg. You fall tonight, that's 100 feet straight down. And I'm not talking about pixie feet. Understood?"

"Yes," Cole said.

"I'm so excited!" Ellie clapped her hands. "And also, yes."

Kevin gave them a small smile and nodded. "Alright. I'm going to release the previous shift. Remember, staple them, confirm the lock on the screen, and send them my way." He hesitated. "Ellie, why don't you follow the first train to the preshow? You should probably see what happens at night."

She perked up. "Are you sure?"

"Absolutely. Just stay on the walkway on the station side. Get ready." Kevin nodded to each of them and struck off. He spoke into his radio. "Open the queue."

"Let's do this," Cole said. "Are you excited?"

"Am I *excited*? Cole, you have no idea."

"I have some idea. You're doing that bouncy leg thing."

Ellie glanced down at her foot, which was, indeed, bouncing. She grinned at Cole and headed to the front of the train, waiting for the first group to clear the queue. Once they were sure the park had sent the humans home, magic started changing everything.

The station widened as she watched, and the bright lights beneath the track dropped away. The nearby tunnel to the preshow shortened and grew rounder. There were other subtle things, things that might be missed if she didn't know what to look for, but Ellie caught a dozen changes that happened in moments.

And then it wasn't just Ellie and Cole in that room. It was foxes and brownies, pixies and elephants, shretma and lanky Fae she had no name for. A jumble of bodies and creatures, many of which were pointing at her.

"Find your seats!" Cole shouted. "It's not safe here, but we can get you out."

The smallest of the Fae headed to the back, where the train now had multiple restraints waiting against a series of stacked seats. The largest guests moved to the center, while the front was a mix, so everyone could enjoy leading the escape.

"They really have humans here, Mom!" one of the foxes shouted.

"And we'll help keep you safe!" Ellie called back without missing a beat.

The fox opened his mouth, but then stepped back closer to his mom, hugging his bushy tail. Ellie assumed commenting on the utter adorableness of the fox would likely be met with the same disdain as Roman complimenting her off-hours wardrobe. You didn't want to hear from a thousand-year-old Fae that you looked *proper*.

As soon as the guests finished pulling their restraints down, Ellie and Cole started at the front. The leather apron and arm pistons of their costumes didn't get in the way as they checked each lap bar and pushed it tighter before lifting up. One after another, it continued, some getting an extra click, others already perfectly snug. The last car with the brownies had a large lever to test all nine restraints at once.

Cole threw a thumbs up and Ellie mimicked it before hitting the launch button. The train lurched forward to the preshow, and Ellie followed it in. It would take a minute for the next train to load, which gave her a chance to watch Kevin's new preshow.

It still looked like the tinker's workshop from the queue, the boom of the failing door echoing through the darkness.

Kevin ran on stage, his leather apron weighed down with far more gadgets and tools than the station ride ops. His spiel was the same. Until the end. "You all made it this far! Can you hear them? The guards are getting close now. Keep your hands and anything else you'd like to keep attached inside the vehicle. Hands up. Head back. Bars down. Hold on to your butts. And take the underground passage!"

The room spun, the track tilting down as a black hole

opened beneath it. The riders screamed as the train tilted forward farther and farther until they locked in at 90 degrees, staring straight into the dark below. Some pushed back on their restraints, trying to claw their way up, while others held their arms straight out. A motor hummed, and the train launched.

Ellie didn't think there was a single rider who wasn't screaming.

"How about *that*?" Kevin shouted.

She clapped her hands. "It's amazing! One day, Kevin. One day, I'm going to ride that thing."

He grinned and waved her on. She sprinted back into the station as the next train of riders got settled, returning just in time to check restraints. Ellie and Cole might not have been as fast at dispatches as some of the regular ride ops, but they were within seconds of the target every time. A few misses here and there due to getting some of the more … unwieldy Fae situated, especially when it involved tentacles, but well within their required times.

In fact, thirty minutes after opening, Ellie and Cole had the queue worked down to the last room. A line so short Ellie herself would have been running back for a re-ride. It wasn't long before the small fox made another appearance. This time, he waited for the front row, but his mom wasn't anywhere to be seen.

He hopped onto the brackets for the restraint and then hurled himself up into the seat.

"Left your mom behind for this one?" Ellie asked.

The fox child laughed. "She looked a little green." He furrowed up his brow. "That's the right color, right? That's what the humans say when you're sick?"

Ellie grinned at him. "Yes, it is. And it's not fun getting green on a ride, is it?"

"No, it's not. I rode the spinning barrels by myself on the carousel! One time, I spun it so fast Mom got sick, and they had to call in a code …" He furrowed his brow. "Green?"

"That's the one," Ellie said with a laugh.

"She must love you telling that story," Cole said.

The fox bared his teeth. "She hates it."

Ellie pulled a small square coupon out of the pouch at her waist. "Hold on to this for your mom. You can get a free snack anywhere in the park. Maybe help settle her stomach."

"Thank you! Humans are great! Well, the ones I've met, anyway."

A low beep sounded when the last restraint came down. Ellie and Cole started down the row, both trying hard not to laugh. They reached the end and Ellie dispatched the train.

She pointed at the screen. "Fifty-five seconds!"

"Let's keep it up!" Cole clapped his hands together.

"BREAK TIME!" KEVIN shouted as they sent another train hurtling down the tracks.

Ellie eyed the queue. "But we still have a line."

"No worries. Fae are generally *a lot* more patient about these things, Ellie." Kevin held out a Ball jar filled with frozen white liquid. "I got you two a treat tonight because I've heard you're doing great."

"And you want us to come work more night shifts?" Ellie tried not to sound too hopeful.

"Maybe I do."

The jar felt like ice in her hand, a wide straw sticking out the top, with the scent of vanilla and honey filling her nose. An irregular nugget of honeycomb candy, sometimes called a molasses puff, garnished the rim.

"I love these milkshakes. Thank you."

"You've never had this milkshake," Kevin said. "I called in a favor. This is cut comb honeydew honey. Richer than what you're used to, but less sweet. Perfect for a honeycomb milkshake!"

Cole took a sip. "You should try that, Ellie."

She did, enjoying the cold after racing back and forth across the platform for the last three hours. The honey flavor was undeniable, an explosion of sweetness without being sickly. Decadent, not very acidic, though that could have been a side effect of the milkshake itself.

Ellie glanced at Cole. "That's incredible."

He frowned at his milkshake before scowling at Kevin. "You're going to ruin me for regular honey. I like my clover honey!"

Kevin grinned at the pair and sipped at his own milkshake. "Glad you like them. Finish those up. Don't forget the molasses puff, and let's finish strong. I want to get through this line as soon as we can at park close. I have a second date and I don't want to be late."

"Second date?" Ellie perked up. "The first one went well, then?"

Kevin swooned. "He's a narrator, Ellie!"

"Of what?" Cole asked.

"Romance books. That voice." Kevin beamed at Cole. "I could listen to that man all night. So, we're getting out on time tonight, right?"

Ellie grinned and nodded at him before pulling the chocolate nugget off the side of her jar. It was an odd candy, easy to bite through the chocolate layer before the airy crackle of the candy inside met her tongue. The light texture hardened as she chewed until it was almost like a caramel. Such a strange blend of textures, and a wonderful mix of flavors.

Cole muttered into his milkshake. "Do you know how wired I'm going to be, Ellie? This is so much sugar."

Ellie answered by taking a long sip of her milkshake, cringing back when the first bolts of brain freeze stabbed at her head. She tried pressing her tongue to the roof of her mouth, which she'd heard was supposed to help, but it didn't stop her eyelid from twitching.

"Brain freeze?" Cole asked.

"Yep." Ellie scrunched up her nose and breathed a sigh of relief as it finally passed. Then she immediately went back for more.

As worried as Ellie had been about taking care of the Fae kids on second shift, it went remarkably well. They had a young kraken who continuously tried to hold his restraint a little higher with a sly tentacle to get more airtime, and a pair of raccoons who literally screamed at each other the entire time, but outside of that, the Fae kids on Tinker's Escape were extraordinarily well behaved.

Ellie followed Cole out back to the employee lockers. She had about an hour before third shift officially got underway, and while cleanup wasn't the most exciting task she could imagine, it would be nice to say hello to some of the nocturnal park dwellers.

"You're really taking a double tonight?" Cole yawned before he finished the question. "That was an exhausting shift."

"Wendy asked, and I need her to help keep the brownies happy, so yes. I'm taking a double. At least it's not a triple!"

Cole shuddered at the idea. "Let's get changed and grab a snack."

"Something small, maybe. I could go for that. I'll definitely be ready for breakfast by the end of third shift. Meet you out front."

Cole nodded and pulled the contents out of his locker before heading for a changing room. Ellie did the same, swapping back into her everyday clothes because the park would be empty. It was the only time Roman let the dress code slide for employees on the clock.

She found Cole waiting outside, a strong breeze catching his hair and blowing it directly into his eyes. He swatted the hair away, blew out a breath, and started down the stone path beside her.

Ellie could just make out the security line, led by Bruce, ushering the last of the Fae guests toward the front of the park. They had it down to a science, and she was fairly sure they could clear the entire park out in about thirty minutes.

"What do you feel like?" Cole asked. "Potato on a Stick is still open. Or we could always get another pretzel. Or the café, if you want something bigger."

Ellie's boot scraped an uneven bit of the path. "Let's do Potato on a Stick. I haven't been there in a while."

"Sounds good."

Cole was easy when it came to picking a place to eat. Ellie didn't think there was a single dish in the park he didn't like. Or at least didn't like enough to avoid it altogether.

There were two Potato on a Stick stands, one ironically placed in the Irish-themed area called Dublin Street, and the other near the mascot meet and greet on the edge of Lost Empire. Since the rear section of the park had already been cleared by security, they headed to the nearest stand.

The intricately paved cobblestone paths gave way to concrete as they reached the exit to Lost Empire. Potato on a Stick sat close to the inner hub, the alternative to Dark Forest's Midwest BBQ stand, which was a popular destination for ribs during the day. And, as Roman put it, extremely rare steaks at night.

Ellie had little interest in finding out exactly what Roman meant by that. Even by human standards, she wasn't a fan of rare steaks. They moved too much like gelatin, which disturbed her a bit.

All thoughts of too-rare meat fled when the slowly spinning potato caught her eye. It was, while not the most creative sign, certainly the most realistic looking. She wouldn't have been surprised to find out it was a real giant potato spinning on a stick.

"Two, please," Cole said at the window.

Franzi shuffled around inside the booth, whiskers twitching as she came back with two large potatoes on wooden sticks. "Drinks with that?"

"Water would be great," Ellie said.

"Same." Cole handed her a potato.

Franzi pushed two cartons of water out the window. "Enjoy!"

"Thanks, Franzi!" Ellie took a deep sniff of her potato and sighed. "I know it's magic, but I still love these things."

"Brilliant, really," Cole said around a bite of potato. "They're cheap, delicious, nutritious, and don't make a giant mess."

Ellie bit into her potato, the texture still a bit toothy, but the taste of butter and salt and bacon all rose together. Warm and rich, parts of the skin cracked like a potato chip. "These are ridiculous."

Cole grinned. "Ridiculously good."

Ellie watched the lights dance around the mascot meet and greet. Beyond, she could see the garden of Titania's Table sitting in the center of the lake. It was a beautiful place, and one she felt she should visit more, but she always got distracted once the food arrived.

"Tottie and Poe were eating these on last night's vlog." Ellie took another bite.

"The Taters were eating taters on a stick? Isn't that like cannibalism?" Cole raised an eyebrow.

Ellie snorted a laugh and pushed his arm. She almost dropped her carton of water, adjusting it and tucking it into the crook of her elbow. She caught the time on the clock at the back of the meet and greet and sighed. "I need to be up front in ten minutes. Better head that way."

Cole nodded as he bit deeper into his potato. "Have a good night, Ellie. I'm going to shower and pretend I'm dead for the next eight hours."

"No, you're not. You're going to be gaming for half the night and complaining about your lack of sleep tomorrow.

We'll see who's more exhausted."

A low laugh escaped Cole's lips. "We will indeed." With that, he offered a warm smile before turning and walking back the way they'd come.

Ellie headed south toward the entrance, enjoying the quiet before the cleaning began. They had a great maintenance crew who worked overnight, but they tended to get a little grumpy without help. And, if she was being honest, a few things were too delicate for them to clean.

And no one wanted a repeat of the great pretzel shortage from two years ago. No one. One thoughtful worker had decided to clean the oven. It had taken a month to get it fixed.

Ellie finished her potato as she rounded the lake, slowing when she heard an angry voice on the wind.

Chapter 9

"*THIS IS WHAT* you do with your life, Roman? You are wasted here with the younglings and the humans. As worthless as a bard on a battlefield."

Ellie had never heard the voice before, but the heat in his words caught her attention. Roman's name piqued her curiosity as she passed the back of the theater where they performed a play about an ancient conflict in Faerie. She stayed close to the wall, decorated in ornate carvings of flowers and vines, framing faux marble statues that Ellie wasn't so sure were faux anything.

She knew she wasn't stealthy enough to go entirely unnoticed by any Fae who was paying attention, but Fae in an argument were sometimes too focused. Ellie took her chance and slipped up to the corner, the voices growing louder, clearly in the entryway for the theater.

"What will you be when the wars are done?" Roman's voice was a whispered barb. "When the fighting is finally over, and the fighting is all you were? What then, Stephen?"

The other Fae's words grew hard. "You go too far, soldier."

"You wish to speak to me as if I am still at war, *General.* For me, the fighting was never all I was. But you have long been death, cousin, and darkness is all that waits for you. If I can bring some small light to this world, I will." Roman's words softened. "May you realize what truly matters before that conflict turns you to dust."

A heavy pause preceded a harsh whisper. "It would not take much for the king to learn of your ruse here, Roman. Tread lightly, or those of us who were your allies will be your end."

"If you threaten my people, Stephen, I will remind you of who I am. A soldier in name, but something more you should not wish to awaken."

Boots scraped the ground. Ellie expected another retort, a harsh word, anything. Instead, there were only rapid footsteps leading away from the theater.

"Ellie."

She bolted upright, her voice cracking. "Yes?"

"Come here, please."

She stepped around a cascading marble fountain at the side of the entrance, butterfly wings guiding the water to the vase below.

Roman didn't look aloof or disengaged from the world. In that moment, he looked sad.

"Are you okay?"

His expression shifted, a small smile on his face. "Of course, Ellie. Now, tell me, what did you hear?"

For only a moment, she thought about denying she'd heard anything. Trying to forget the conversation and letting Roman do what he needed. But she didn't want to lie to him. He'd taken her in, given her a place to live after some of her darkest days. Become a guardian when so many others had failed her.

Ellie rubbed her hands together and met his gaze. "I heard you talking to Stephen. It sounds like he's a general you used to fight for? Or worked for? I don't know how that works in

Faerie."

"There was a war, Ellie. For some, there is still a war that rages in the emerald fields. A place to which many Fae claim to have rights. War is not something I wish to be a part of." He made a sweeping gesture to the park. "This is what I wish to leave to the world. An escape. A place where dreams are something that walks beside you, and not things that wither unfulfilled."

He didn't meet her eyes for a time. "What else, Ellie? What else did you hear?"

"I … I heard him threaten you. To tell a king about you? Or what you're doing here?"

Roman inclined his head. "We are tricksters at times, as you well know."

"That's pretty obvious."

A smile flitted across Roman's face. "Yes, I suppose it is. Tell me, how many stories of Faerie do you know?"

"After working here? A lot. My mom used to tell me a bunch, too, when she was still alive. Irish fairies and Scottish fairies and all sorts of wonderful tales."

"They are not all wonderful, Ellie. There is a darkness and warning in many of the stories you know, and many you have never heard. And with good reason. Fae can be every bit as treacherous as humanity." He looked away for a moment. "You know there are stories from many places, Fae of many kinds. It is one reason we have Dublin Street beside reproductions of the Fairy Glen from Scotland. We have had kings and queens, legacies and tragedies, who have marched through the ages. Not all are benevolent. Many I would not call good. Others have stories that remain untold."

"Not so different from humans, then."

"Why do you say that?"

Ellie shrugged. "Before we had books, I mean. There must be so many stories we lost. I still have pictures of my parents. My grandparents, even. But before that, the names are hard to remember, and another generation before that?" She shook her head. "Stories no one remembers anymore."

Roman slowly crossed his arms. "I see the parallel, Ellie. Your lives are so short here. I never gave it much thought, to be honest. But it does ring true." He paused before reaching out and squeezing her shoulder in a rare physical show of support. "I will always do my best to keep you and everyone else in this park safe. *You* have more stories to tell, Ellie. And I look forward to hearing them."

She hesitated, then gently touched his forearm. "You're okay, Roman?"

"I will be, Ellie. There are forever storms on the horizon, but we will weather what we must." He adjusted his hat and walked away without another word. Some of the Fae were like that. When they'd finished talking, you'd know because they simply left.

Chapter 10

ELLIE WALKED TOWARD the entrance arches, glancing over at the Fairy Glen and Dublin Street beyond. She'd heard several humans complaining about Irish and Scottish attractions being in the same theme park land, but it hadn't struck her that the Fae themselves rarely complained.

She'd seen the Blue Men of the Minch chatting with mermaids and selkies, brownies and pixies sharing a meal with Cait Sith. It was a terrible thought to imagine any of those wonderful beings trapped in a war in another realm.

Roman's calm demeanor had cracked ever so slightly. Ellie had never seen him upset before. It unsettled her more than she'd expected. But she also trusted him, and learning something of his past would not easily break that trust.

"Third shift open!" Bruce called out from the gates.

The wall next to Ellie unfolded, rough stone stretching out to reveal layers behind it, scraping and grinding until a figure sat beside her. One of the many Norse golems who sheltered at the park.

"Clear!" the golem called out in a booming voice.

More and more sections of the wall shifted and grunted and eventually stood, or at least sat up. Some of the golems were no taller than Ellie, stout and broad, while others loomed taller than Roman himself.

The nearest rubbed his head and looked at his fingers. "Is that …" He patted his head again and cursed in disgust. "I've gum on my head, Mundi. Who goes around sticking gum on peoples' heads? I'll bet Thrud and Yngvarr don't have gum stuck to them, do they?"

A shorter golem, built of many round stones, raised his foot, bending his knee at an angle impossible for humans. "Got plenty of it on my feet too, Sindri. Likely those bandits again."

"Bandits?" Ellie asked.

"Aye, bandits. You call them raccoons."

Ellie bit her lips. She was fairly sure the raccoon-like Fae were used to being called raccoons at this point, but it still made her want to laugh that the golems were calling them by that name, too.

Mundi reached out and grabbed a trash can, the creature lurking inside shrieking with excitement as it moved. Ellie wasn't sure what actually dwelled in the depths of the cans, but Cole said she *really* was better off not knowing. Sometimes curiosity almost got the best of her, but the haunted look in his eyes when he spoke of them held her tongue.

Exaggerated chewing sounds echoed out of the void when Mundi flicked the gum into it. The park stayed remarkably clean most of the day, as the cast members were trained to toss any trash they ran across. It kept the cans fed and happy, and it kept the park looking spotless.

Ellie grabbed a long trash picker from the concealed maintenance closet beside the Fairy Glen. It reminded her of a claw toy she'd had when she was a kid. The trash picker worked much better, thankfully. With that and a paper bag in hand, she started around the far side of the land, heading west into

Merrows Lagoon.

It wasn't a simple paper bag, of course. When it came to Roman, little was ordinary. The bags never leaked and never smelled, an enchantment Ellie greatly appreciated.

Tentacles the size of tree trunks rose from the water. An intimidating sight until one noticed the gentle care the kraken took to reorganize the pedal boats. She might be a key feature of Kraken's Fury, certainly one of the best flume rides Ellie had ever been on, but the fantastic animatronic Roman had installed could be swapped out in minutes for shift change or any unforeseen need.

Ellie waved to the nearest mermaids tying the pedal boats down for the night. They returned the gesture before dipping below the lake's surface and vanishing without a trace.

The boats bobbed in place, the sleek visage of a kelpie carved into the bow of each. Its face reminded Ellie of a dragon crossed with a horse, scales tracing the boat's length until it reached a curled tail.

She plucked a crushed popcorn bucket from the path and dropped it in her trash bag. Third shift wasn't the most exciting time in the park, but it was nice to see the golems out and about, not to mention the kraken and the more mischievous pooka.

Ellie continued around the outskirts of Merrows Lagoon, weaving from one side of the path to the other as she left the dock for the pedal boats behind. Soon enough, the tall, thatched roofs of Merrow's Feast and Ocean Treasures, the land's main restaurant and retail shop, came into view.

The staff milled about inside and along the dock that stretched into the lake, helping with cleaning and finishing one more important meal for the night. Two carried an enormous stewpot between them, a high-pitched whistle echoing through the air. One of the kraken's great eyes swiveled toward them before she reached out with a tentacle.

Ellie watched as the kraken took the stewpot and tossed the contents into its fanged maw, gently handing it back to the staff and waving before moving north in the lake. Only when the kraken had returned to cleaning the lakebed did Ellie focus on her task again. Focus was a hard thing to come by when some of the park's denizens were about.

She didn't find much in the way of litter close to the restaurant, so she continued on to the rear of the Kraken's Fury ride backstage. Out of sight of the guests, and rarely visited by the park's supervisors, the break area got a little messy.

A small channel of water flowed through the back of the tiered mountain, ending in a pool for the mermaids to relax in without having to don their human forms. It was a thoughtful addition by Roman, but one thing he hadn't considered was the snacks. Or, more importantly in that moment, the remnants of the snacks strewn about the shore.

Lobster shells and fishbones waited patiently to be collected in the sand pails around the edge of the small lagoon. Not a lagoon, exactly; more like a hot tub. One that the mermaids occasionally invited the other staff to enjoy. Ellie had gone a few times, but the mermaids always liked to tell scary stories, and *that* didn't make for the most relaxing evening. Though she was happy to endure a little fright for the sake of entertaining her friends.

Ellie wrinkled her nose at the last pail. Gus had said they planned to install a trash can near the backstage pool, but it still hadn't been done. Normally, the shells were cleaned out every day, but some had clearly been missed. She dropped the pail's pungent contents into her trash bag and moved to the next.

"Thanks, Ellie!" Shay, one of the mermaids, called out from the entrance to the ride.

"No problem!" Well, with an enchanted trash bag that masked every smell inside, it was no problem, but if she'd had to smell that lobster shell much longer ... Ellie scraped her tongue across her teeth.

She finished her loop around the backside of Kraken's Fury, exiting the employee path onto the main entrance walkway used by guests. It ran alongside the lagoon's edge, and she found herself right beside the kraken once more.

Ellie's pace slowed. The water from the lagoon had shifted south, rising above the banks, and pushing the pedal boats into the air. There were times it was easy to forget some of the magic that flowed through the Theme Park at the End of the World. This was not one of those times.

A Fae stood on the docks, arms raised as if holding a great weight. While the water rose in the south, the levels dropped along the north, revealing the algae-covered basin of the lagoon. With two long swipes of her tentacles, the kraken cleared huge swaths of the algae away, sparing enough for the resident fish and the things the fish fed on to be satisfied, but creating a crystalline view into the depths.

With one section done, the distant Fae shifted her arms, and the water flowed away from the ride, exposing another patch of the lagoon's basin. The kraken repeated her swipes, leaving the bulk of the algae near the center to dwell beneath towering kelp blooms.

"Ellie?"

She jumped at the mention of her name. Her head snapped to the side, and she found Ana standing beside her, close to the entrance to Merrows Lagoon.

"Hi, Ana! What are you doing here?"

Ana flashed her a brief smile. "Closing down the restaurant takes some time. I heard one of the water witches was here and came to watch." She gestured to the Fae standing on the docks.

"She's a water witch?" Ellie had heard the name before, but she didn't know much about them. Some of the Fae weren't spoken of at great length to humans. Even those humans they trusted.

"She is, and it's not a common sight. I'd love to know how Roman got her to agree to help out here from time to time."

The waters of the lagoon shifted again, the kraken moving closer to the witch as their dance continued. A swell of water, a swipe of tentacle, and a graceful shift of an entire lagoon.

"She hasn't spilled a drop, has she?" Ellie asked.

Ana let out a low laugh. "No, Ellie. They are powerful beings. Best not to cross them."

"Which is totally different than every other powerful being I work with."

Ana patted her back and smiled. "Touché, as the humans say. Touché, Ellie. You know, we have a new lobster bite dish coming to the table."

Ellie glanced at her trash bag and tried hard not to make a face. Apparently, she failed.

"Not a lobster fan?" Ana's brow furrowed.

"I am! But maybe not tonight."

Ana frowned, looked at the trash bag, and then gave a slow

nod. "Ah, cleaning out the hot tub?"

"Yes," Ellie said with a hiss.

Ana laughed in earnest. "The joys of third shift. Just be glad we don't have to climb down into the lagoon and squeegee the entire basin. *That* used to be awful."

"Down *there*?" Ellie pointed to the kraken and the waiting algae.

"Oh yes. We'd block the water, drain it, and those of us with no talent for dice rolling would lose nearly every time. The worst part was falling down. In my head, I knew it was just algae, but it's so … slimy." Ana shivered. "Blech."

"Not the good old days?"

"No, Ellie. Definitely not." She grinned at her. "Try not to get too bored on third shift, will you? I'll see you around."

"Have a good night, Ana."

Ellie stayed and watched the water witch and the kraken for a short time before heading for the central hub. There she found the golems again, tending to the landscaping by the lakes and paths.

Mundi muttered to himself. "Gum on my feet, gum in the trees, gum in the … why does Roman allow this? It is an insult."

"At least you didn't have to clean out the chum buckets," Ellie called over her shoulder.

Mundi harrumphed. "She does have a point about that, doesn't she?"

Ellie worked her way through the paths in the Dark Forest, not finding much in the way of the litter there. She looped past the land's barbecue restaurant and skimmed by Town Square and the mascots' meet and greet. Two of the pooka walked the grounds, one bouncing on his feet and waving as the other stared off into the night. Ellie waved back.

She continued into Lost Empire. The food stand next to the Puffing Demons had been a great idea on one hand, a convenient snack for those entering and leaving the land. But allowing food on the antique cars had not gone well.

The track was often strewn with napkins and empty popcorn buckets, even skewers from the potatoes on a stick. *No gum, though*, Ellie thought as she plucked up her second popcorn bucket and an empty cup. She'd always thought the worst of the litter came from the daytime guests, but judging by the violent orange stains in the popcorn bucket, some was from the Fae hours.

Ellie enjoyed spicy snacks, but an entire bucket of Carolina Reaper popcorn wasn't fit for a human palate. She walked the grounds, under the bridge where the wind tended to deposit the lighter trash, and cleared out what little she found. All in all, it was fairly clean already, which gave her a chance to admire the ancient city skyline built at the back of the ride.

Forced perspective gave the skyscrapers a towering appearance, brick and brass and copper accents peppering the smaller structures in front on the slowly looping track. It wasn't the most exciting ride in the park by any means, but Ellie loved the steampunk elements in the scenes and the animatronics along the way.

Huge steam engines sat beside mechanical animals. Essentially, exposed animatronics with more copper in them than steel. Of course, with a park full of Fae, iron and steel were in short supply where they could be reached by a guest.

Ellie pushed deeper into the land, passing the Airships

queue and the entrance to Tinker's Escape. By the time she made it to Howling Mountain, her shift was almost done. Five more minutes, and she could clock out and climb into bed before the next day's shift after a whopping six hours of sleep.

Her phone buzzed, and she pulled it out to check. A message from Capy waited on the screen.

Capy: *Important. Come by guest services before your shift, please. Nothing bad, so please do not worry.*

Sometimes, Capy knew exactly what to say to make Ellie worry.

Chapter 11

T HE MORNING ALARM came far too early for Ellie's taste. She shuffled off into the shower, the hot water tempting her to stay home even longer, but Capy's message stuck in the back of her mind. Ellie threw on a pair of cargo skorts, one of humankind's greatest inventions, her last good bra, which meant laundry day was coming, and a dark blue, collared shirt common among employees who weren't working an attraction at the moment.

She reached for her gray running socks and slipped them on before tying up black tennis shoes. Some of the Fae liked to wear formal shoes for work, but their feet didn't get destroyed by walking tens of thousands of steps in a shift.

Ellie grabbed a cold brew coffee out of the fridge and chugged it. That would have to do. Hair mostly dry and shoes on the right feet, she hurried down the stairs from her apartment, crossing over into the stone, castle-themed floors of the building before setting out into the park.

She went left when she reached the central lake, cutting across the bridge to Titania's Table. Halfway around the inner path, Ellie stepped onto an unmarked gravel trail winding between the Dark Forest and Merrows Lagoon. It bypassed the main walkways for the rides in either land, eventually meeting up with flagstones and finally concrete as the HR building came into view.

Raised voices were clear as the birds in the nearby tree. And one of them she recognized.

"Gus, no. This isn't the first time this happened, and I know better than anyone here how to deal with them."

Ellie cracked the door open in time to see Gus slap his paws on the desk. "That isn't your choice, Cole. Roman decides how we approach this."

Cole had lived at the theme park so long, Ellie sometimes worried he'd lost touch with some of his more human skills. Like being subtle instead of blunt and expecting everyone to simply accept what he'd said at face value. He'd been better lately, but she could see Gus was frazzled.

"Ellie," Capy said, drawing her attention. "Please, come in and have a seat."

Wendy's trunk hovered above the cubicles in greeting before she stood up herself, pushing a large office chair around the corner to sit between Capy and Gus.

"What's going on?" Ellie asked.

Capy slowly scratched her nose before wiggling it. "Well, we have learned there will be an inspection today. The DFS Amusement Ride Safety team will be here late in the morning."

"DFS? Like the Division of Fire Safety? As in *human* inspectors?"

Gus threw his paw out toward Ellie. "*See.* Ellie gets it. This is *important*, Cole."

"We normally have some notice of what they intend to look at." Capy shuffled the papers on her desk. "This is different. We do not know which attractions they wish to inspect, though considering the department, it is likely one of the coasters."

"They looked at the coasters in the spring." Cole crossed his arms. "They aren't going to look at them again already."

"Nevertheless, I want to be sure every ride is prepared. All after-hours features need to be hidden. Anything that may be safe for Fae but not for humans *must* be concealed. It is Roman's instruction, and that is the instruction we must follow."

Cole dismissed the idea with a wave of his hand. "We'll do what the boss says. Got it."

Ellie frowned at him. She wasn't sure what was wrong, but something was definitely bothering Cole. It wasn't like him to be that callous, and it bothered her to see him like that. "Capy's just telling us what Roman wants, Cole. It'll be fine. We can go out for lobster bites when we're done."

Gus chittered. "You've been talking to Ana, haven't you?"

"Maybe a little on third shift last night."

Cole blinked and uncrossed his arms. "You worked that late and now you're already here. I forgot … I forgot about that. Did you get enough rest?" He leaned a little toward Ellie.

"I'll be okay. Let's just get through these inspections, and then I can worry about resting some more."

Wendy held out a tablet held with her trunk, showing a balding middle-aged man with bushy eyebrows and a graying beard. Her voice sounded like one of the recorded safety briefings every employee had to watch during orientation. "This is Karl. It's our understanding he's the inspector coming today. They rarely come alone, as these safety protocols are taken seriously. But remember, it's Karl who makes the final call on everything. Be sure he's happy. Be kind to him. Do not offer to buy him anything. The inspectors don't take well to any amount of perceived bribery."

Ellie thought about asking how Wendy knew that, but in the end, thought it better to let things lie.

A low ding sounded and a message popped up on the tablet. Wendy turned it around and her eyes widened. "It would appear our inspectors are early. Roman says they're asking to see Gowrow's Cave."

Capy gestured to them. "Ellie, head to the ride. Cole, please join Kevin at Tinker's Escape to make sure he is prepared should the inspection spread."

"I will." He wrung his hands together as he stood up. "And I'm sorry. I really didn't think they'd be looking at the coasters again already."

"It's okay, Cole. Let's focus on making this go smoothly."

He nodded to the trio at the desks, smiled at Ellie, and headed out.

"You'd best be going too, Ellie." Gus tapped his wrist as if he were wearing a watch, which he wasn't. "Time is short."

ELLIE BARELY HAD time to walk the track at Gowrow's Cave once before her phone dinged.

Roman: *Meet us at the ride entrance.*
Ellie: *omw*

She cringed after she sent the response. It was easy to forget Roman hated any kind of abbreviations in a text message, but it was second nature to use them. She could practically hear his sigh from the other side of the building.

Ellie increased her pace, staying on the walkways and steps

normally reserved for ride evacuations. One train roared past her, heading deep into the underground cavern at the climax of the ride. She loved the sound of that coaster: a rumble like a distant thunderstorm, joined by a chorus of happy screams.

The light of the tunnel brightened, and Ellie was back at the far end of the platform. Themed to a convenience mart in the middle of nowhere, it was an oddly charming station. She stepped through the next ride vehicle that pulled to a stop, slipping past the few guests who had come to Gowrow's Cave at rope drop. Most people ran for Tinker's Escape, which was a strategy Ellie definitely agreed with. It got the longest line in the park, though there was something to be said for lapping Gowrow's Cave over and over.

Out in the better-lit areas of the queue, Ellie hurried at a pace just below a jog. She cut through the single rider line, which reduced the trek by quite a lot and missed the better parts of the theming.

She saw Roman and Karl before she heard them. The owner of the park looked his sharpest, top hat on his head and perfectly pressed jacket forming tight lines around his narrow frame.

"Here she is now." Roman gestured to her. "Ellie, I'd like you to meet Karl and his assistant."

A young man with a clipboard inclined his head, but didn't speak.

Karl glanced at him with some annoyance. "This is Juan. Forgive him. He rarely stops taking notes. Great employee, but not the most talkative."

Juan rolled his eyes while Karl wasn't looking.

"Nice to meet you both."

Juan didn't offer more than a small wave in response.

Karl nodded. "Thank you, Ellie. Now, I understand you have a coaster that jumps the tracks? I don't know how I didn't notice that at this year's inspection, but it doesn't sound safe."

A light laugh escaped Roman's lips. "Gentlemen, no. It's a false track. I assure you no wheel leaves the ride's actual track. Allow me to show you."

He led the way into the queue. The first room looked like the foyer of an elegant cabin in the woods, but they barely made it into the second. There, the queue exited out the far side into a dimly lit walkway made to look like little more than a dirt road. But Roman instead gestured to a door just inside the second room. "This will take us to the lower levels where you can see the entire mechanism, including the hidden track."

Ellie didn't miss Roman's subtle hand gestures and whispered words as they walked down a hallway she swore she'd never seen before. She had no doubt part of what she was seeing was an illusion, but her eyes couldn't pierce it. No theming waited in that place, only the void of light and the LEDs along the baseboards to show the way.

They turned a corner to the left and there were the tracks, running through the underground cavern. Ellie was positive that hall hadn't been there before.

"Let me know if you need more light to work. If we'd scheduled this during off-hours, I could have cleared the tracks completely for you."

"It's no worry, Roman." Karl clicked the button on a heavy flashlight and shined it at the steel structure. Two separate tracks appeared in the beam.

"Ellie, please explain the layout for our guests."

"Umm … sure, Roman." She glanced over the dual-layered track and figured out quick enough what Roman was doing. "As you can see here, the cars are always elevated a bit." A train roared by, vibrating the lower track and the walkway beneath their feet.

Ellie pointed to the upper track. "If you follow this one, it's clear where the false breaks are, arching up over the gowrow's head." The animatronic moved slowly, following the intense airtime hill that normally wasn't attached to a thing.

But now, where the track separated, a lower track could clearly be seen pulling the ride back down. "And when you're on the ride, you can't see the lower track at all, thanks to the lighting and the wide nose of the train."

"Thank you, Ellie," Roman said.

Juan glanced from Karl to Roman. "Is that the only break in the tracks?"

"It is, yes."

"I'd like to see it for myself," Juan said.

"From the ride?" Ellie asked.

Juan nodded. "I told Karl he didn't need to do a surprise inspection here. This park isn't some lazy Photoshop job on a viral video thumbnail."

Ellie suddenly liked Juan quite a bit, and she began to suspect why he hadn't spoken. He was waiting for the perfect time to throw his boss under the bus. Or train, as the case might be.

"We should ride it together," Ellie said with a quick glance at Roman. The sooner they left backstage, the sooner Roman could drop the current illusion. "So they can get the best view of the track."

"Of course. Let's return to the station for a proper ride."

Roman turned on his heel and led the way forward.

Ellie just made out Karl's whispered comment. "I don't want to ride this thing, Juan. I hate roller coasters!"

There was more than a little amusement in Juan's quiet laugh.

But Ellie had another question she didn't yet have an answer to. Could Roman maintain an illusion like that from the station for the entire ride? His next words confirmed her worry as they stepped into the station.

"Allow me to remove my hat." Roman placed it gently on the shelves normally reserved for water bottles and other staff essentials.

Ellie didn't miss the stress and hesitation in Roman's demeanor. She could try to buy him more time, or at least keep him out of sight of the inspectors while they rode.

"Mind if I ride with you in the second row?" Ellie asked.

Roman cast her a small smile. "Of course not. Let us leave the front row to our friends. They should have the best view."

Juan turned and winked at Ellie and Roman. Apparently, he was happy about his ruse to get his boss on the ride. Roman let out a long sigh as they seated themselves in the second row, goosebumps rising along Ellie's arms.

"I love that you're still using an old tire launch on this coaster," Juan called out from the front row. "LSMs are nice, and I like a good hydraulic launch, but something about the tires just speaks to me." He paused and looked at Karl. "Are you praying?"

Ellie barked out a short laugh before biting her lips. She pulled the overhead restraint down and adjusted her position in the seat before clipping the seat belt to the harness.

With the restraints locked, and belts buckled, the attendants started down either side of the train, checking each row, and buckling the empty seats closed. Ellie wondered if the inspectors would find it odd that Roman didn't sit in the front with them, considering there were four seats to a row, but Juan just looked excited to be riding. And Karl looked terrified.

"One of the best coasters in the state, Karl!" Ellie shouted as the train released and slid forward, a quick dip in the track before they reached the tire launch on the sharp incline of the lift hill. It started out slowly at first, giving the audio time to engage.

"Save the cryptids you can, friends. We have two young gowrows in the back of the train who need sanctuary. Take the road through the cave and get them to safety! But beware the darkness, as dangers hide around every corner. Legend tells of an ancient gowrow with the power of a dragon, but they haven't been seen in a century."

Ellie gripped the handles on the harness hard because she knew what was coming. What she didn't know was coming was the high-pitched squeal from Karl when the tire launch engaged, and they shot forward. Climbing a lift hill gradually built tension and anticipation but being thrown to the top of a 150-foot hill in a heartbeat, only to be forced into an intense barrel roll, crushed that tension and anticipation into a single second.

The track veered to the side, dropping low against the ground before taking a sharp turn, looping back, and punching into the daylight. Ellie shouted with joy as the train rose higher, twisting left into a cobra roll before straightening out and diving like a rock on a steep slide.

Ellie put her hands in the air as they shot back into the darkness of the building. A moment of weightlessness as they rose through a loop. She knew the track well enough to grab hold of the handles and push herself deeper into the seat as they reached the bottom, inertia forcing them into the seats hard.

The train didn't slow, but the course took a slow turn to the left, giving them their first glimpse of the boneyard below. The skeletal remains of a hundred different creatures had been cast and painted to appear as real as possible. The onboard audio engaged again, the low rhythmic beats growing louder, as if a great creature were stalking through the cave.

"This doesn't look good. We gotta get out of here!"

A loud boom echoed around them as the track corkscrewed, and then dove straight toward the boneyard. It was a simple illusion. The angle of the props made the ground seem impenetrable, until you were suddenly passing through the tunnel.

Karl barely had time to scream before the train rose again. Juan laughed beside him, arms held high as they swerved left and then right before hitting a short brake run before the final helix.

Ellie glanced at Roman. He no longer had his eyes open, fingers moving in a hypnotic series of flourishes as his jaw flexed. She'd been through the jump on Gowrow's Cave dozens of times. Maybe hundreds. She knew the ride couldn't exist as it was without magic, but seeing Roman *use* magic to hide that fact from the inspectors was both amusing and a terrifying display of power.

There was no penetrating what she saw with her own eyes,

despite the fact she knew what was around them. The audio engaged again, and she knew exactly where they were, exactly what they should have been seeing.

"Look at that beast!" The lights brightened on the massive animatronic, her head rising until her eyes were even with the train. A rumble filled the room as the tail of the gowrow lashed out, prompting a panicked response from the narrator. "The cave's collapsing! Brace yourselves! We have to jump!"

Karl shrieked.

Juan howled with laughter.

Roman clenched his fists and eased them forward, and Ellie watched in awe as a dual-layered track appeared below, just visible beneath the sheared-off steel, as if it had always been there.

They hit the opposite side of the gap as smoothly as ever. An impossible feat made almost routine by Roman's illusion. He released it as they exited the helix and took a banked turn into the final brake run.

"Well done, friends. You survived, and now those cryptids can live in safety."

Karl's knuckles were bright white on the restraints in front of them. He didn't let go until they came to a stop in the station and ride ops instructed everyone to unbuckle and wait for the harness to rise.

To his credit, Juan didn't laugh. Much.

Chapter 12

ELLIE FOUND HERSELF in Odin's Hall with the inspectors and Roman. Nestled between the hills separating Howling Mountain's rides, the soaring timber-heavy building never failed to inspire. The hall interior stood adorned with banners and shields, with the kitchen exposed where a head table would normally sit.

Roman sipped on mead poured from an opaque bottle. "It is quite divine if you would like to taste a glass. A true experience worthy of Valhalla itself."

Karl shook his head. "We're still on the clock for another hour. Bad enough I'm letting you buy our meal."

"You already submitted the inspection, my friend." Roman dismissed the thought with a wave. "It matters little what I offer you at this time."

Ellie rubbed her hands together when the server came by, sliding a flat rye sourdough bread off a soapstone baking plate and onto a wooden serving dish. The first time she'd tried it, she'd expected a hard, crusty thing like a normal sourdough. This was anything but.

"Do we just use our hands?" Juan asked.

"For the bread." Ellie nodded. "I'd recommend a knife for the butter."

Juan tore a piece off and put it on his plate before reaching for the butter. Ellie did the same when Karl declined.

She buttered the bread and bit down, enjoying the light crunch and char from the wood fire that gave way to a buttery-rich tang from the sourdough. The only thing that could make it better was honey, which she knew would arrive by the end of the meal.

"Do you have more inspections this week?" Roman asked.

"More than you might think." Karl took a long drink of tea. "The local fairs start up next month, and we'll be all over the state. That means we have to finish hitting the big parks that are due for inspections within the next two weeks."

Juan tore off another piece of bread. "And none of them have bread this good."

Their server returned, bowls balanced on a tray as he handed out porridge topped with pork and onions, steam curling up from the dish. Ellie's mouth watered as soon as the rich smells reached her nose.

Karl leaned over his dish and took a deep breath. "I have to admit, Roman. You have some of the best food I've ever tasted. I don't just mean for a theme park, either. Haven't seen porridge like this since I was in Europe."

Ellie remembered friends in high school who almost gagged at the mere mention of porridge, or oatmeal, or anything they considered "sludgey." Ellie had always thought it was a little ridiculous, but everyone had different tastes. She also figured they'd never had the porridge at Odin's Hall because it was one of the best dishes she'd ever tasted.

Warm oats and barley sat beneath fatty pork, contrasting with the snap of seared onions and herbed broth. There wasn't anything quite like it at the human restaurants she'd been to, though Roman swore it was a traditional preparation even the Vikings would have enjoyed. Either way, it was delicious.

Juan held up his spork. "I like the utensils."

Ellie raised an eyebrow and looked at Roman, waiting for him to meet her eyes. He didn't, so he missed the mischievous grin on her face. "You know, when Odin's Hall first opened, they only had knives and spoons."

Roman sat his utensils down and laced his fingers together, apparently realizing the error of his silence.

"It was only two years ago I convinced them to get *some* kind of fork. You know, even if it's a spork. Sporks aren't traditional, of course." She gestured to Roman. "And Roman wanted everything to be authentic to the time period it represented. But forks? I think it's okay if we modernize the utensils a bit, don't you?"

"Ellie," Roman said, a hint of amused warning in his voice.

She grinned at him. "I'm just saying I like the sporks."

Roman sighed and picked his spork up again. "I admit they are quite convenient."

"And less messy."

"How would you eat the meat without a fork and a knife?" Juan asked.

Ellie wiggled her fingers. "Ever been to that restaurant where they pretend you're at a medieval jousting tournament and serve you a whole chicken with no utensils?"

"I love that place!" Juan pursed his lips. "I guess it wouldn't be so different from that."

Roman gave Ellie a slow glance. "Of course, the Vikings still had knives and spoons, Ellie. So much of the meat would have been cut up beforehand to cater to the appropriate utensils."

"And then it would all dry out." Ellie frowned and stuck her tongue out just a little at the idea of dry, disappointing pork.

Karl laughed and dug into his porridge.

They ate in silence for a time, Juan clearly enjoying the sourdough flatbread as he finished the first serving, and the kitchen sent him another round. Roman sipped at his mead, offering it to Karl once more.

Ellie couldn't be sure, but it looked like Roman was wearing the inspector down. Even if he didn't give in and try it today, she thought he'd likely be visiting the park as a guest. Though probably not riding Gowrow's Cave again anytime soon.

Juan sifted through his porridge, savoring a large bite of pork before gesturing to the bowl. "Roman, what else is in this? I'm familiar with the oats, but there's something more to the base, isn't there?"

"Barley." Roman inclined his head. "Roasted to provide a nutty flavor. I am quite fond of it myself. Though, prepared poorly, it can be rather bland."

Karl's fingers moved across the face of his phone fairly quickly for an older person. He poked at it a few more times before tapping on the table with some impatience. A moment later, his phone dinged, and the man visibly relaxed in his chair.

"Juan, looks like we have the rest of the day off."

The younger inspector leaned back in his seat. "Did you just call in for us so you could try the mead?"

Roman already had his hand in the air, gesturing for the server.

Karl grinned at Juan. "Maybe."

ROMAN AND KARL finished a bottle of mead between them, and Ellie was quite sure Juan would be driving after that. Mead had a stronger kick than a lot of folks realized, and Ellie had seen more than one visitor find themselves in trouble at the bar. They had shuttles for the guests when such occasions arose, but it wasn't uncommon for Roman to request and comp a rideshare for those who needed it.

He took care of his patrons, both human and not-so-human.

This was all secondary to the dessert now being placed in front of Ellie. She rubbed her hands together and picked up a spork. Pancakes soaked in honey weren't the best option for finger food. She'd be sticky for hours if past experience had anything to say about it. No matter how long she scrubbed, it felt like she'd missed a sticky spot.

"How are you still hungry?" Karl asked, staring at Juan.

Juan paused with a quarter of a folded pancake in his mouth. He shrugged and chewed the bite. "No mead, and this is delicious. You need to try the honey. What kind is it?"

"Heather honey." Roman offered a small smile. "Perhaps not exactly like the Vikings would have had, but it is close. I feel that is acceptable considering our … sporks."

Ellie snorted a laugh and bit into her pancakes. A little dense, but the texture made it feel more decadent than it really was. A good chewiness complemented the honey permeating every bite, giving it a slightly salty, almost malted flavor with lingering caramel notes.

They finished dessert, and Ellie felt ready for a nap. Which would probably be on the schedule if she didn't get moving again soon. Thankfully, Karl took care of that concern.

"About time to be going, I think." Karl tapped his watch. "I do appreciate this, Roman, very much. It's been nice learning a bit more about your park." He leaned in conspiratorially. "And your mead."

Juan patted the older inspector on the back before turning to Roman. "I'll get him home safe. But like he said, thank you for lunch. I've never had anything quite like it."

"Of course. You are welcome to join us again in the future. After the inspections are complete, of course. I wouldn't want our socializing to appear … unseemly."

Roman pushed his chair back, and that was all the signal the group needed. They stood and headed down the long tables toward the front door.

"Come, Ellie. Let us walk our guests to the gates."

"I need to stop by Titania's Table on the way," Juan said.

"Oh?" Roman waited for him to explain.

"For an empanada. Best I've had since my abuela passed. Don't tell my mom." He flashed a huge grin at Karl.

"Fine, fine," Karl muttered. "I'm in a good mood."

Juan placed a hand over his heart. "The rarest of things."

ROMAN TOOK A deep breath and let it out slowly as the inspectors left through the front gates, to-go container piled with empanadas in hand. "I must compliment you on your help today, Ellie. I feared my illusions may not be enough to fool them. Enough that in the future, we may rebuild the ride in the same fashion you witnessed today."

"Happy to help. You looked a little stressed, so I just tried to buy you time."

"Time was all I needed. I had not considered taking the inspectors on the ride itself. It was a brilliant idea, Ellie. I only needed to cast an illusion for the time we were in the cavern itself. The same section of the ride we revealed beneath the earth."

"Was that easier? Because you'd already conjured it?"

Roman pondered that question for a time. "I am not certain, Ellie. It still required focus, a level of concentration that would make it far more likely to answer an inspector's question incorrectly. And changing the mind of one so certain as Karl is a terrible amount of effort."

"You mean wiping his memory?"

"That is a simpler thing. I mean truly changing his mind. Altering a memory of what he saw, so that he never again questions what he saw. That is both nuanced and difficult. And should we have failed that inspection … I shudder to think what the insurance rates would have done."

"You're welcome." Ellie flashed him a broad smile. She paused. "If you're worried about the rates, couldn't you just make gold? Some Fae must be able to do that, right?"

A small smile lifted the corner of Roman's mouth. "No, Ellie. That would be … unsportsmanlike, as the humans say. You would have to pay the Fae guilds for a boon such as that, and they don't take money."

"What would they take?"

Roman hesitated. "Sometimes I find it odd to be discussing Fae matters with you, Ellie. But you have earned my trust, and that is no small thing. So, understand when I tell you this is something you must not reveal to another human."

"I won't. Not a word."

"Good, walk with me." Roman led her away from the gates, angling toward a mostly vacant walkway in Carnival. "For an exchange such as what you mentioned, it would require a hefty bounty. Tantamount to a changeling payment, a trade of lives."

"That sounds a little extreme."

Roman harrumphed. "Extreme, yes, that is a good word for it. There are times you find a willing trade. A changeling who wishes to remain in the human lands, who only needs a fool of a Fae to strike the bargain. I know of one such bargain, Ellie. One where the Fae did not realize the family they meant to infiltrate had long since been lost. Those were darker days."

"What happened to the changeling?"

"The changeling? They were able to live the life they wanted. But the Fae who failed to provide to the guild? Imprisoned or executed, most likely. A deal is a deal, as it were."

Ellie shuddered at the idea, curiosity almost prodding her to ask for details, but common sense won out. An unkind Fae was pure nightmare fuel.

"Do not worry much about such things, Ellie. Perhaps you would instead like to visit Carnival to try the new food Hans is working on."

Ellie narrowed her eyes. "No churros."

Roman released a low, hesitant laugh. "No churros."

Chapter 13

CAPY PULLED ELLIE out of ride ops at the beginning of the summer. It wasn't terribly unusual for Roman to want Ellie supervising the setup of the seasonal events, but she was woefully uninformed about what might make suitable fare for Corn Dog Crave Days.

She'd managed to get a playlist from the Taters about their favorite corn dogs, so Ellie had spent the weekend reviewing several episodes of Poe awkwardly stabbing himself in the mouth with a skewer. One thing she knew for sure was that there was going to need to be some Korean corn dogs on the menu. They looked amazing.

While the idea of getting that arranged might have been exciting, dealing with the shretmas about their retail plans was quite the opposite.

"Bro, no." Manfred gestured to the wall of mascot plushies. "These are too nice, Katinka. We can get these for half, no, a quarter of the cost."

Katinka scoffed, her whiskers vibrating. "You're out of your mind, bro. Already cheap. You want to give guests pooka-shaped trash?"

"Yes, bro. Yes!" Manfred turned to the plushies and stretched, his low pants revealing a stubby tail on the swath of exposed back fur.

Ellie pinched the bridge of her nose. "We aren't replacing the prizes with junkier prizes, Manfred. Roman already said no to that." She waited a moment. "Bro."

"Bro!" Manfred placed a paw over his heart. "Straight to the heart, bro."

Ellie checked the time on her phone. She was supposed to fill the shretmas in on some other bad news, but it felt like something way above her pay grade. She took a deep breath.

"Two other things. One, Roman wanted you to follow the script, but we're still getting complaints about the rude comments."

"*Funny* comments!" Katinka protested.

"Not funny to everyone."

"Bro." Katinka crossed her arms.

"Not funny to anyone." Roman's voice caught Ellie off guard, and she jumped.

"When did you even get here?"

"Just now, of course." He turned his attention to Manfred and Katinka. "I understand you called a child ugly."

"Yes, he was hideous! All human children hideous, bro." Manfred's mouth twitched with a smile.

Ellie didn't completely disagree with that assessment. Every time someone said, "Look at that adorable baby!" she generally thought they looked like a wrinkly bundle of dried meat left too long to rehydrate. But that wasn't something you *said*.

"We had to comp their tickets and food for an entire day, Manfred. And was that in the script? Was insulting our guests anywhere in the script?"

"No, bro." His long nose turned down.

"But the script ..." Katinka started. "Bro, it's like a robot talking."

Roman eyed the shretma. "We are going to try something new. Enough of our guests have asked if you are animatronics—though an animatronic could *certainly* follow a script better—that you're going to *be* animatronics now. Sell it. Minimal responses, friendly smiles, slow, precise movements."

"Bro!" the shretmas whined in unison.

"And if I hear one more whisper about identity theft or credit card fraud from *any* of the shops, there will be consequences."

Manfred let out a long sigh and waddled over to the register. He pulled something off the card reader and pocketed it.

"Don't forget the other register, bro." Katinka gestured to the far side of the counter. "And the reader at the security gate."

"I'll get it, bro," Manfred muttered. "Robots now, are we? Boring, bro."

"One other thing." Roman waited for them to meet his eyes. "Stop saying bro so much."

Manfred's nose wiggled in absolute annoyance at that suggestion.

"What did you decide about the plushies?" Ellie asked. It was a sharp barb after Roman's declarations, and she knew it. But it was probably the best chance she had of getting them to do the right thing.

Manfred sighed. "Getting some better quality, bro. Nice plush for the guests. Best quality we can get."

"Best quality we can get and still profit on," Roman said. "Balance, Manfred. Always look to keep things in balance. And remember, while Ellie is acting supervisor, you answer to her. I will support her decisions and any disciplinary action she levies against you."

"Working for humans," Katinka said. "Weird park, b—Roman." She caught herself before she said bro again, but that was a habit that would take a very long time to break.

They were almost out the door when Roman glanced back. "I do not want to hear another whisper about identity theft in this park from anyone. Should it happen again, you will be speaking directly to Bruce, and I will make sure he is in a *very* bad mood."

The horror-struck faces of Manfred and Katinka were something Ellie wouldn't soon forget.

ANOTHER DAY PASSED and Ellie's mind wandered back to the question about why Roman put up with hustlers and employees who wouldn't shy away from a scam. Maybe it was something from their past, or maybe it was simply a mutual respect for other Fae. Or at least the craftiness of those other Fae. She didn't know, and she wasn't entirely sure she wanted to know.

Her mind soon shifted to other thoughts when she caught sight of the signage and decorations that had been installed overnight. Corn Dog Crave Days looked like it was going to be the equal of the biggest festivals in the Theme Park at the End of the World.

A promise of fireworks and snacks and memories to last a lifetime. Ellie would have to compliment the creative department. She'd been worried the decorations wouldn't be ready in time for the passholder previews, but the staff had pulled together and set the stage.

Food booths waited around the central lagoon, at least one in each land, and of course multiple in Carnival. How could you only have one corn dog stand in a land called Carnival?

Red, white, and blue stars and banners flew above the food booths, oversized fireworks and rockets looming over every stand. It certainly made them hard to miss, and Ellie smiled at the level of detail the artists had incorporated into the smoke.

LEDs flashed at the base, faint in the daylight, but it would be brilliant at night, making each rocket look like flames were rising. Ellie had a moment of concern that one of the Fae might conjure *actual* fire for the rockets after hours. That was probably something she'd need to bring up before the festivities began in earnest.

She passed the Dark Forest and its barbecue corn dog stand before noticing the Korean corn dog stand by Merrows Lagoon. On the sign, an excited tiger held a corn dog in one hand and a bottle rocket in the other, each ridiculously oversized, but adorned with simple, smiling faces.

The menu caught her eye. Corn dog garnished with diced french fries, battered, deep fried, drizzled with truffle sauce and greens. Ellie almost had to squint to see the greens. She blew out a breath and muttered to herself.

"I know where I'm sending the Taters first."

She wasn't sure how authentic truffle sauce was, but the second corn dog sounded much more traditional. Coated with gochujang mayo and fried ramen noodles, the second option sounded just as good.

"Hi, Ellie!"

She turned toward the voice and found a pair of alligators walking upright, tails dragging the ground behind them as they waved with their short forelegs.

"Mateo! Valentina! I didn't know you were back for the season."

"Roman called us in a little early to cover some PTO on Kraken's Fury," Valentina said. "A bit chilly compared to the Everglades, but I think we can survive. Now, where's my hug?"

Ellie grinned at the gator-like Fae and stepped closer, dodging a mouthful of teeth before wrapping her arms around the rough scales and getting crushed by gentle claws. She did the same with Mateo.

"Are you working today?"

Mateo nodded. "Back on Kraken's Fury first thing. They're moving the animatronics out now. I don't know how well I can pretend to want to eat people, though."

Ellie frowned at that. "Why?"

Valentina let out a laugh. "Gus. He just fed us about ten pounds of birthday cake. And no, it's not our birthday."

"That squirrel has a problem." Mateo patted his stomach. "Well, we better get in position before the gates open. It's good to see you again, Ellie."

"You, too!"

Ellie continued on through Dublin Street, where a booth selling a hilariously inauthentic corned beef corn dog was adorned with a leprechaun fit for a cereal box. Sometimes she worried the Fae were simply trying to make each other angry. She'd once heard Kevin go on a five-minute rant about how corned beef wasn't even an authentic traditional Irish dish.

She glanced at the line forming outside the gates. Passholder previews were going to be big this year. Ellie had tracked the views on some of the biggest channels for vloggers, and she'd never seen views so high for the Theme Park at the End of the World. There was another half hour before they opened, and the ticketing queues had already reached capacity.

Past Carnival, with a corn dog stand that looked straight out of the state fair, right down to the field of lightbulbs in the flashing sign, Ellie found Howling Mountain's stand. While she might have had an idea of where to send the Taters first, *this* was now her priority.

Grillpølse, wrapped in chorizo and jalapeños before being dredged and fried. Now that was a proper snack for a long theme park day. She rubbed her hands together and continued around the central lake, passing through the edge of the land and into Lost Empire.

A humble corn dog stand waited there, simple in appearance with no more than an antiqued poster with a faded image of a corn dog on a stick and the price. But Ellie knew what they were using for the meat in that stand, and it wasn't what she thought of when she thought of corn dogs.

Fish sausage was the highlight at the innocuous-looking booth, and Ellie wasn't entirely sure how she felt about it. There were many seafoods she'd grown to love over the years, from fish paste to anchovies, but sausage just felt a little out there. It might be a one and done, but she was determined to try everything.

Across the walking path waited a new booth. An aged patina framed a sign with a simple name: Toymaker. There wasn't a counter to keep guests outside of it. Instead, an open spread of shelving and awnings funneled the guests straight to the workshop in the back.

Ellie made her way inside when she heard something clatter

and thump. She paused when she saw the top hat on the counter and the tall Fae grunting as he tightened a series of hoses to a metal block.

"Roman?"

He turned, wiping sweat from his brow. "Ellie! Welcome."

She hesitated and cocked her head to the side. "What … what are you doing?"

"Visiting an old hobby of mine."

Ellie leaned on a stack of crates, frowning at the array of pistons and vats and various molds. "What is all of this?"

He wiped his hands on a rag and set it next to a block of metal. "Some of the tools I used for casting armor in another life."

"Armor? You made armor? Like a blacksmith?"

Roman inclined his head. "An apt description, though there are other *considerations* with making certain Fae armors."

"Magic."

"Indeed, Ellie. But as I said, that was another life. One I have no wish to revisit if it can be avoided."

There were times Roman said something so casually that Ellie would almost miss the warnings behind the words. He'd grown more forward over the years, but now and then he'd still slip in something like that. Such a small phrase, with unknowable consequences.

"Do not worry over such things, Ellie. I did not mean to concern you."

"That obvious?"

He offered a smile. "Only to those of us who have been around humans for great lengths of time." He gestured to the assembled hoses and molds. "I have repurposed these to create something else. Have you ever come across little plastic souvenirs in your travels?"

"That's … a little vague, Roman."

After a short pause, he elaborated. "They create figures and sculptures from plastic by injecting the material into molds."

"Oh, yes! I used to have a penguin from the zoo, as a matter of fact. But I thought that was wax and not plastic."

"Perhaps it was in that time, Ellie. I planned to demonstrate how tin could be cast into souvenirs, but the iron content is high enough to be a danger to some Fae."

"Capy shot you down?"

A small laugh escaped Roman's lips. "Indeed. So, this is my solution instead. A way for the guests to interact with us and create a souvenir."

"It looks complicated, Roman. Who's going to run this thing?"

"I am."

Ellie blinked. "For both shifts?"

He answered without hesitation. "Yes." Roman threw a switch that looked like something straight out of a Frankenstein movie. Two large gears shifted against the back wall, and the first of a series of bulbs lit.

Roman tapped on the lights. "At least three of these need to be illuminated to ensure everything is hot enough." He moved to the opposite side and spun a valve handle that was at least as large as a steering wheel. "This is cold water. It will only reach the mold once an adequate amount of plastic has been injected."

"So, it's molten plastic being forced into the mold instead of metal?"

"Exactly." Roman tested one of the lines, moving it up and down and stretching the coil before nodding. He sat the contraption on the counter, sliding it into a bracket before gesturing to it. "This runs the actuator that forces the plastic through. Give it a try."

Ellie grabbed the handle and pulled it toward her. It wasn't difficult to move, exactly, but there was a good amount of resistance. Some kids might need a hand from their parents. "Will it get easier when there are more lights?"

Roman glanced at the bank of bulbs. "Yes, it will. But this should be good enough for our test."

The handle reached 90 degrees, and then Ellie could put her weight into it. It stopped at a deeper angle.

"Perfect. You can release it now."

As soon as she did, something clicked in the base of the lever, and it slowly rose to its starting position.

Roman put an ear to the mold and smiled. "Still works. Wonderful. When you released the handle, the water flowed into the metal. See the condensation here?" He gestured to the water gathering on the outside of the mold halves.

"How hot does that get?" Ellie wondered just how danger-ous having the mold exposed was.

"Hot enough. A human would not want to touch it." But Roman laid his hand on it with abandon, holding his palm up afterward to show Ellie he was unharmed. "That is why we have the counter here, to keep away those susceptible to it."

A puff of steam curled away from the mold and he slid another lever to the side. The metal halves split apart, revealing a plastic mascot with a large corn dog in hand. Roman pulled a third lever, and the plastic popped off its base. He lifted it and handed it to Ellie.

"Still warm!" She moved it back and forth between her hands. "Roman, this is adorable. It even has the name of the park on the base! I love it." Ellie studied the holes in the bottom and the detail on the face. Only then did she realize which mascot it was. "The tiger! With the hot dog. This is amazing."

"Corn dog," Roman corrected.

Ellie gave him a flat look. "Of course."

He held his hand out for the figurine, turning it when Ellie returned it. "Each week will have a new mold. One for each of the booths. I remember you telling me how humans like to collect sets of things."

Ellie laughed. "That's really smart, Roman. People are going to love it. You should put a sign up that shows what—"

He pointed to her left before she finished speaking. A poster with six different figurines of various colors and shapes stood out on the shelf.

"Touché."

A chime sounded, and the park's morning announcement came to life. "Welcome, guests, to the Theme Park at the End of the World. Please enjoy your stay, and remember, the park will be closing at 8:00 this evening."

Ellie rubbed her hands together. "I'm going to head up front, Roman. The crowd waiting at the gates is huge."

"That is good to hear. When you have finished greeting and welcoming our guests, I would appreciate feedback on the corn dog booths."

"As in tasting them?"

"Yes."

"*All* of them?"

"In time, Ellie. Do not injure yourself in the name of corn dogs." He delivered those sage words without a hint of irony.

Ellie still laughed. "Thanks, Roman. And by the way, I love this booth. The Toymaker thing you have going? It's really neat."

Roman gave her a wide smile, a rare expression to be sure, and she was happy to see it.

"ELLIE!"

She looked around as she worked through the throngs of guests flooding into the central hub. Someone grabbed her arm, and she turned to find Cole, dressed in khakis and a dark blue, collared shirt much like hers.

"Cole, you're supervising today, too?"

He nodded. "Yes, but I wanted to tell you I saw the Taters coming in the front gates. Thought you might want to say hi."

"Thank you!" She clapped her hands, smiling at a family as they walked past. "I would. And Roman wants a report on all the corn dog booths."

"All six of them?" Even Cole, with his limitless appetite, looked intimidated.

"Want to split some with me over lunch?"

"That sounds like an excellent idea. I'm introducing the gators to some of the newer mermaids at eleven, so find me at Kraken's Fury when you're ready."

"Will do."

With that, Ellie set off toward the front gates again. If she knew the Taters—and at this point, she felt like she did—they'd likely be headed clockwise around the park, which meant their first stop would either be Dublin Street or one of the stands deeper in the park. Considering the crowds, Ellie figured they'd be farther back.

She took the bridge to Titania's Table and, from there, took the path toward Merrows Lagoon. The crowds thinned out when she turned right, cutting north past the Korean corn dogs and spotting a familiar pair of space buns entering the Dark Forest.

Ellie hurried forward, dodging a family taking photos across the lake, making sure not to photobomb them. She was at the edge of the Dark Forest soon enough, the bizarre sign for the barbecue corn dog booth catching the sunlight on silver and blue strips of reflective ribbon.

Poe had his camera angled at the ground, a sure sign they weren't filming, and they certainly weren't livestreaming anything. If Ellie remembered correctly, their next livestream wasn't scheduled until tomorrow, anyway.

Ellie tried to lower her voice and imitate Bruce as best she could. "You have a permit for that camera?"

Poe spun in surprise, one hand already raised to start explaining before Tottie burst into laughter.

"Oh, Ellie, I haven't seen Poe that distressed in a long time. Thank you."

Poe patted his chest before narrowing his eyes and glancing between Tottie and Ellie. "You're both evil. But at least Ellie gives us good information."

"I do enjoy being your informant." Ellie grinned at them. "But it looks like passholder previews might have gotten a little more exposure than I realized."

"Imagine that," Poe said, slowly turning his gaze on Tottie.

She stared at the ground.

Ellie leaned over until she could look her in the eye. "Something happen?"

"I might have let something slip about it in our monthly chat."

Ellie raised an eyebrow. "Is that the one I missed? How many people were on the chat?"

Poe started counting on his fingers. "Let's see. Three, four, five, about a thousand."

That certainly helped explain the hordes waiting for the park to open. "I'll let Roman know you helped today be a massive success. I'm nudging him to do more events, like the media events some of the other parks do."

"Oh, Ellie, that would be amazing! You think he'd invite us?" Tottie clasped her hands together.

"I'm pretty sure you're the only vloggers he knows the names of. Unless he's been doing research I don't know about or talking to Cole, but all of that seems pretty unlikely."

"Have you tried any of the corn dogs yet?" Poe asked.

"Not yet, but Roman wants me to try them today. See what I think. I think he's trying to kill the entire staff with corn dogs."

"Worse ways to go," Poe said solemnly.

Tottie sighed and rubbed her forehead. "That's my husband."

"Did you see the corn dog stand closer to Merrows Lagoon?" Ellie asked. "I wanted to be sure you got over there because it's garnished with diced french fries and then the whole thing is deep fried and drizzled with truffle sauce."

Tottie's eyes got a little bigger with each word. "Are you

joking? That's next, Poe. I don't care if it's going backward. I want french fries on a hot dog with truffles. Truffles. Ellie, are you serious?"

"It's a sauce, but it looks like there are some pretty decent chunks in it."

"We're getting this barbecue monstrosity and heading there. No arguments."

Poe didn't argue.

The line didn't take long to get to the barbecue stand. Ellie grinned at Hans when she saw his barbecue sauce-stained paws.

"What can I get you, Ellie?"

"Let's split one," Tottie whispered.

"Two corn dogs, Hans."

"Two dogs!" Hans shouted as if there was an entire line of cooks waiting to fill the order. Instead, he opened a smoker and pulled out two skewered corn dogs by the time Ellie finished paying. He leaned out the window, handing one to Tottie and the other to Ellie.

"You enjoy those now. Burnt ends in a Kansas City sauce. A little sweet, but we should have some mustard sauce later if you want some variety."

"Thanks, Hans!"

"Have fun today!" Hans waved to Tottie and Poe as they thanked him.

Ellie led the way back onto the path. "I got two so we can eat one before Poe lets the other one get cold."

"You're a genius." Tottie held the second corn dog out to Poe. "Get the video, will you? I'm going to eat."

"Yes, captain."

"Are you sick?" Tottie asked.

Ellie shook her head.

"Excellent. You bite first. I don't mind sharing. Poe can have the cold one." She flashed a wide grin at Poe. "The price of taking the photos."

Ellie bit the end off the corn dog. She wasn't sure what she'd expected, but crisp batter that gave way to fatty, salty pork with a burst of sweetness from the sauce certainly wasn't it.

"Oh. Oh wow. I didn't think this one was going to be that great." She took another nibble and handed it over.

Tottie eyed the skewer, then bit it from the side, pulling the length of wood out before chewing. "Oh, what?" She talked around a full mouth, cheeks puffing out a bit. "There's cheese, too! Cheddar? What? This is ridiculous."

"Now that was a good reaction." Poe lowered his camera.

"Did you just film me stuffing my face?"

Poe shrugged. "You were on the same chat I was. They love that. Well, most of them, except that one guy who thinks every meal should be eaten with a crab fork."

"We don't talk about him."

Poe whispered to Ellie. "It's her cousin." He finished two more clips of the corn dog before taking a bite himself, clearly enjoying it as much as Tottie had. The second bite, he yelped.

"Did you just stab yourself in the mouth?" Tottie asked. "Again? What is it with you and skewers?"

"I don't know. Let's just go get the potato thing, yeah?"

Tottie grinned at him. "Good idea."

"You need to go see Roman while you're here," Ellie said. "He set up a souvenir booth and is running it himself in Lost

Empire."

"Seriously?" Poe asked. "The owner of the park is working a booth?"

"I love this place." Tottie smiled at him. "We're definitely stopping by. Do you think he'd let us film?"

"He might! Just ask, and tell him who you are." She held a hand up. "Actually, I can walk you over there later."

"That would be great, Ellie."

Soon enough, they were in line for the Korean corn dog stand. It wasn't as short as the barbecue line, but it wasn't as busy as Ellie expected, either. She wondered if the hordes were still at the front of the park in Dublin Street and Carnival.

Some of the Fae might have complained about the corned beef corn dogs, but the locals sure wouldn't. Every time corned beef was on special at Titania's Table, they sold out. Every. Single. Time.

"So, what have you two been working on lately?" Ellie asked.

Poe let out an exhausted sigh. "Trying to come up with new games for the channel. Everyone seems to like the coin flip the most, but we can't do that *every* week."

"You still haven't done trivia," Ellie said.

Tottie shuffled forward as the line moved again before turning to Ellie. "Everyone does that, though? Even our favorite channels do that."

"Maybe because it's fun?" Ellie raised an eyebrow.

Poe opened his mouth to respond, closed it, and looked at Tottie. "You know, Tater Tot, she may have a point."

"Trivia." Tottie rubbed her chin. "Alright, maybe we'll try it. We could source questions from subscribers."

"I can help you with some obscure park trivia!" Ellie said. "Stuff neither of you will ever get right, and you can't even search for it because no one knows."

"I like that idea a lot," Tottie said.

Another guest finished checking out, and the line shifted forward, close enough to read the menu, which immediately distracted the Taters.

Poe gestured to the sign. "You didn't exaggerate at all, Ellie. That thing looks amazing. Are we getting two of them again?"

"Yes," Ellie and Tottie answered in unison before breaking down with a laugh.

"How are we going to eat this thing? You know how big a mess that's going to be, covered in sauce and chunks of fries?"

Tottie pulled on Poe's sleeve as a guest walked by. "See the tray? I think we'll be safe."

Poe blinked.

It wasn't long before they were at the window and checking out before one of the slibreg Ellie didn't know handed them a pair of corn dogs. Ellie thanked them and waved before making two rapid clicks with her tongue behind her teeth.

The slibreg paused, whiskers twitching, before returning the sound with a shallow nod.

"The costumes here," Poe said as they wandered away. "I'll never get over it. And like, what are they?"

"Giant rats?" Tottie asked.

Poe shook his head. "Rats don't have furry tails."

"The costumes are *very* well maintained, aren't they?" Ellie said. "I think they're more like gerbils."

"Either way, they're adorable. Almost as adorable as the mascots, if you ask me." Tottie led the way to a bench on the edge of Merrows Lagoon, overlooking the water. "Come on, Ellie. Let's eat this while it's hot."

Tottie took the first bite, her brow wrinkling as she slowly chewed from one side to the other before sinking back into the bench. "That's … I'm not even going to give you a hint. Try it."

Ellie took the corn dog, checked how deep the skewer was, and bit a good-sized chunk off. The first thing that struck her was how crispy the potatoes were on the outside. An extra crunch with the already crisp batter. But all those thoughts fled when the earthy notes of the truffle sauce took over everything else.

It only lasted for a moment before the snap of the corn dog and rush of flavor from the meat and cheese rose to balance out the entire bite. If it wasn't Tottie and Poe sitting beside her, she would have unceremoniously devoured the entire thing.

"That might be the best thing I've ever had on a stick."

Poe snorted a laugh as he set his camera down and took the tray from Ellie. This time, he went at the corn dog from the side, which, while he avoided trying to give himself an impromptu piercing, left him with truffle sauce smeared across his cheek.

It was quite the look when he sat there speechless, staring at the corn dog.

Tottie took that moment to take a quick video of his messy face. "That's going in the vlog."

Poe handed the corn dog back to Tottie. "All I'm saying is I'm glad we have two. That's magic. That is corn dog magic."

Chapter 14

THREE WEEKS OF Corn Dog Crave Days passed by in a blur. Every day felt busier than the last, and Ellie had never seen a food-centric event at the park attract so many guests. The days were packed with humans, and she hadn't seen so many Fae in the park at night before.

The previous weekend ended with three stands selling out of corn dogs, which Roman found entirely unacceptable. Ellie had seen the delivery come in the night before, and she suspected the theme park wouldn't run out of corn dogs before the corn dogs expired. She was also happy to see more vegan corn dogs for Carnival, as those had been far more popular than Hans and Franzi had expected.

But none of that mattered in the moment. Ellie and Cole had a day off, and that meant they were going back for some of their favorite corn dogs and a few rides. Normally, they'd grab brunch at Titania's Table for a breakfast quiche and ill-advised morning milkshake, but today was about corn dogs. So many corn dogs. Even breakfast corn dogs.

Cole finished his half of the Korean corn dog and sighed. "I don't know if I like the overly cheesy bites or the overly meaty bites more."

"All the bites more."

He frowned at Ellie. "That doesn't even make sense."

She took a slow bite without breaking eye contact, making it as awkward as possible. "All the bites."

Cole snorted a laugh and offered her a napkin. "It's an oven out here today, Ellie. You know what that means?"

"I don't want to get wet first thing in the morning."

"It's like third thing in the morning, at most."

She shook her head.

"Come on. I'll sit in front of you, and you can duck. We haven't ridden in months!"

Ellie glowered at him. "You know what happens when I duck! They'll find me, Cole. They *always* find me."

One thing she'd learned about mermaids that she certainly hadn't known before actually meeting them, was many of them were tricksters. Tricksters wasn't even the right word. They were more like pranksters who adored a good practical joke. And if they thought for a moment you didn't like getting wet, well, they were going to work on that like an overzealous therapist.

Ellie led the way. Cole had a few good points. It *was* a hot day, and if she was going to get sprayed with cold water, today was the day to do it. She didn't know how some folks managed to ride Kraken's Fury in the dead of winter. Ellie thought it was cold enough at the height of summer.

Cole nearly skipped along the path beside her. It was a rare day he talked her into a water ride, and she had to admit seeing him so excited almost made getting soaked worth it.

"Have you ridden it this year, Ellie?"

She shook her head. "No, not since I lost the coin flip last fall, I don't think. Wait, no, once this spring? But it was just for an inspection, so most of the water features were off."

"That's cheating."

"Well, it's certainly drier." Ellie laughed and elbowed him as the path turned into cracked flagstones when they neared the entrance.

Kraken's Fury might not have been her favorite ride, but the mountain façade towering over them made an impression. The vivid greens of the valleys rose to blend with the dark gray stone, making the flumes themselves appear to be mountain streams.

Ellie knew the actual ride was anything but a calm mountain stream.

Deep drums sounded in the entrance tunnel as they funneled into the queue, like a booming march pushing them along. Ellie wasn't sure if she was more excited to see the line wasn't long, or disappointed she'd be getting soaked even sooner.

Beside them stood a beautifully carved wall showing ancient fishing vessels surrounded by merrows, deep shadows cast by strategic lighting. People fished in the shallows and greeted them, selkies waiting in the distance, and what could have been mistaken for a mountain loomed in the background.

The next hall revealed maps and charts straight out of an old pirate movie. Fantastical sea monsters circled in red and framed by skulls and crossbones. One map, upon closer inspection, showed a sailing marked out from Iceland to Ireland, and in the center, the same shape of the looming mountains in the queue. A hint of the kraken waiting inside.

One thing that never disappointed was the station for Kraken's Fury. Themed to an old boatyard, heavy timbers and hulls enclosed the space as guests queued up in between them.

Rope as thick as Ellie's arms secured some of the structures while the sounds of hammers and saws and creaking wood were piped in along with the pulse of an ocean bay.

The ride boats squeaked as rubber bumpers hit the brakes when they floated back into the station, now empty but for an intimidating amount of water on the seats. Ellie blew out her breath as they waited for two cycles, then moved up to board.

"Last row," Cole said as they stepped down into the boat. "Sometimes the least-wet spot."

The boat swayed beneath their feet and Ellie sighed as she sat down.

"Don't grab anything or it'll grab you back!" the ride ops shouted. It was one of Ellie's favorite safety spiels, if she was being honest, and considering the number of cast members in the ride at any given time, practical advice.

The boats had three rows that could fit three people across, though ride ops rarely stuffed three people to a row unless the park was excessively busy. As it likely would be later that day.

Two of the ride ops exchanged a thumbs up and the brakes hissed as they retracted, letting the ride vehicle float forward with the current.

"No poncho?" Cole asked.

"In this heat? I'd rather be soaked."

"I'll remember you said that."

Ellie snorted a laugh and scooted up closer to Cole. She could at least keep half of herself dry.

"You know you secretly love this ride."

"No. But I *am* excited about getting some more corn dogs after this."

The flume dipped down, sending a small pop of water over

the edge of the boat as the narration started overhead. "More reports of a giant creature in the sea, close to Rockall, headed our way. This is your one and only reminder. We're to confirm its presence and location, then return to port."

Ellie slid back in the seat when they hit the base of the lift, the conveyor dragging them up the inside of the mountain at a steep angle. Projections above showed a gorgeous sunrise cresting the distant waves. A short time later, they tilted forward and splashed down a small hill into the highest flume.

Light shone in the distance, opening onto the first scene. Emerald green plains stretched out before them, broken up by hills and stones on the right, while the left gave the illusion of an endless sea. Shadows swam in the water, launching arcs of water over the boats at irregular intervals and occasionally hitting riders square in the face.

Ellie knew the water cannons were supposedly randomized, but she'd never felt like that might actually be true before Cole took a stream right to the head, and she stayed relatively dry. Cole spluttered and wiped at his face before the narration started again.

"Rough seas ahead. Hold on."

That was all the warning they had before the first drop, a sudden lurch that pointed the bow down at a 45-degree angle. The riders in front of them shrieked as the beautiful scene turned to a turbulent gray storm cloud.

They splashed down into the bottom, and water cannon or not, everyone in the boat was soaked as water came over the sides.

"It's warm," Ellie whispered in confusion. She caught Cole's grin.

"Told you some things had changed! Roman had heaters installed."

Ships bobbed and shuddered in the storm on the second level. Flashes of lightning arced across the ceiling above, lighting the water of the flume and giving brief glimpses of a shadow in the distance on the wall. The first of the mermaids popped up alongside the boat, and Ellie grinned when she recognized Shay.

"You have to leave these waters! The kraken has come for all who dared steal fish from the sea!" Shay dove into the water and swam away. Ellie knew what was coming, but it didn't make the water any less wet when the cannons fired from their right, operated by that same mermaid.

She didn't miss the laughter coming from the shadows as water dripped down her face.

The next drop in the flume wasn't as long, but it took them outside, the sunlight blinding in the sudden change, but the heat felt quite good in their soaked state. They followed the gentle curve into the next scene, the boat's guide wheels thumping against the flume before darkness fell around them, and they saw other boats in far worse shape. Not much more than splinters and broken masts stuck out from the water now as they drifted amid the wreckage.

Mermaids swam in and out of the ruined ships, rescuing sailors where they could, leaving them heaving on the stones and broken hulls. They all froze at once, turning toward the far side of the scene. It was uncanny and incredibly creepy, and that was before the narration kicked in again.

"It's too late!" the captain shouted. "The kraken has us!"

Ellie screeched as the flume dropped out from under them,

leaving them to get soaked under a waterfall before they were launched into the final scene. Drop tracks were evil. Drop tracks on a water ride were the sort of evil only a Fae could come up with.

There was only one line of discernible dialogue as the water cleared and the true magnitude of the scene opened before them.

"It's the kraken!"

Gone was the gentle creature who helped dock the pedal boats at night and cleaned the lagoon. Instead, replaced by a towering form, the kraken whipped tentacles the size of tree trunks around the room, hoisting shattered boats above its great maw, ringed with rows of teeth like hooked spears.

The room thundered when the kraken's tentacles slapped against long sheets of metal hidden in the darkness above. There was no need for other sound as the kraken thrashed in the water, displacing towering waves to crash over screaming and delighted guests.

And Ellie.

Nothing but chaos and water reached their ears until the boat slipped into the tunnel at the opposite side of the room, and two mermaids popped up nearby. They swam beside them in silence for a moment.

"It was a nest!" the first mermaid said. "Did you see? If only the fishing boats avoid the area, all will be well."

Right as she finished speaking, the boat dove down the final drop, spraying water across everyone inside, as if there was a single dry spot left on any of them. Ellie caught the flash of the ride photo and hoped she'd made a respectfully horrified face as she threw her hand over Cole's mouth in "terror."

Every rider broke down in laughter as the boat hit bottom, slowly circling the flume outside before it drifted back into a cave toward the station. Only then did the narration pick up again.

"A rare sight, baby krakens. Remember this day, friends, and help protect those who need it most."

And in the troughs running down to the station, two tiny krakens appeared. Too excessively adorable to be real, but it didn't stop a boat full of drenched riders from melting over them.

"Family dryer?" Cole asked as they drifted back into the station.

Ellie narrowed her eyes. "If I have to chafe, you have to chafe."

Cole burst into laughter and offered his hand as he stepped out, pulling Ellie to the station walkway. They waved to the ride ops as they left, heading down the exit tunnel with a new map painted on the walls. One that showed the kraken's home as off-limits to fishing vessels, and a new course plotted through the seas.

The only sound outside of the gentle crashing of the waves was a simple melody played on a cello, one that rose and fell with the ebb and tide of the water. It was a beautiful place, and one Ellie likely would have enjoyed a lot more if she wasn't drenched.

They followed the damp footprints off the ride, which led them south toward the land's main gift shop and quick-service restaurant.

Cole waved his employee card at Ellie as they came closer to the family dryers. "We have time."

"Fine, yes, let's dry off a bit." She led the way into the contraption, a dark green and brown plastic shell that faded into the shrubbery.

A quick beep after a swipe, and Cole pocketed his card, stepping inside next to Ellie. "Ready?"

"I just hope it's not as hot as I remember."

That was the last thing either of them could say at a volume less than a scream. The fans kicked on, and it felt like a jet turbine had suddenly started up all around them. Ellie's hair blew straight back, her park T-shirt and cargo skort literally snapping in the wind.

Cole didn't fare any better, stumbling to the side when he failed to brace himself in the hurricane-force winds. Mercifully, the fans quieted a short time later, though everything else sounded muffled when they stumbled out of the dryer.

Ellie straightened her clothes and pursed her lips. "That actually wasn't too bad."

"No chafing for us today." Cole grinned.

"That remains to be seen." Ellie looked around, gesturing to the swarm of pedal boats on the lagoon. "You think it's busy today?"

Cole shook his head. "Roman will be happy, though. And that's a good thing, isn't it?"

"He does sign our paychecks. Come on, let's see how bad the line is for the corned beef corn dogs, then go see Roman."

THE LINE WASN'T exactly short for the corn dogs, but the staff moved at speed. Soon enough, Ellie and Cole had a corned beef corn dog in hand and were walking around the path through

Carnival, headed toward Howling Mountain.

"This is ridiculous." Cole gestured to the corn dog before handing it back to Ellie.

She smiled and took another bite, tart sauerkraut and corned beef sausage wrapped up in a crispy batter and capped with gooey mozzarella. Cole was right. It was ridiculous.

"Ridiculously good." Ellie grinned and handed it back to him. "You finish it. I want to stop for a chorizo and jalapeño corn dog."

"The Grillpølse in Howling Mountain?"

Ellie nodded. "After we see Roman."

"It's a good day, Ellie. Really good day."

She agreed. They matched their pace as they crossed through Howling Mountain, dodging excited families rushing to the rides with the lowest wait times. Listening to others complaining about how full they were, but not wanting to cancel their reservations. That was relatable.

Soon enough, they entered Lost Empire, and Roman's booth had one of the longest lines in the park. It didn't seem to bother the Fae, though. Quite the opposite, as he wore a wide smile on his face as he helped two kids create a molded figurine.

Bruce stood at the back of the line, telling people they'd have to come back later, as even the owner needed a break from time to time. Much to Ellie's surprise, he was fairly nice about it. A little direct, perhaps, but much nicer than she would have expected.

She didn't miss Bruce bristling when one of the guests got a little too close to him. Ellie hurried forward, cutting in front of the security guard as the woman asked a question.

"Can you tell me how to find the theater? I heard there's a wonderful play about this park."

"Closer to the park entrance," Bruce said through gritted teeth.

"Did you walk by Carnival?" Ellie asked, drawing the guest's attention.

"I did walk through Carnival, yes."

"It's just past there on the way back. Look for the building with the large pillars out front close to Fairy Glen and you'll be there."

"Thank you, dear. You should think about working here yourself!"

Bruce eyed the family as they walked away, relaxing as they got farther from his personal space. He glanced at Ellie but didn't say anything about her interfering. No thanks, but more importantly, no complaints.

Ellie and Cole waited for the line to die down, families and older single folks molding their own figurines. More than one reminisced about their childhood collectibles and even things they'd seen at their relatives' homes in display cabinets.

Roman finally worked through the end of the line and waved Ellie and Cole over before drawing the curtain across the booth. "Is something wrong? I saw you two standing there for quite some time."

Cole shook his head. "Ellie wanted to say hi and see how the booth was doing."

"Kind of you, Ellie. Quite well, as you can see."

"Glad to hear it." Ellie bounced on her heels. "Think you'll do this again for another season?"

"I definitely will. It is … nice." Roman wiped his hands on a towel before checking the levels on the vats of plastic. "There is something I need to talk to you two about. I must speak to everyone, but you in particular."

Generally, when Roman said he needed to do something, it was either very good, or very bad. Ellie hoped it was the former.

"There are some things you do not know about the arrangement I have with Faerie. Why they leave us be, here, in this park."

Cole clenched his fists before rubbing the back of his hand.

"Is everything okay?" Ellie asked.

Roman gave a small nod. "For now, yes. One of the generals I served with will be coming to the Fae hours tomorrow. In this realm, his name is simply Stephen."

Ellie tried to hide her reaction, but clearly didn't quite succeed.

"You remember him from his previous visit?"

"I heard you talking to him in the spring. During third shift one night."

Roman glanced at Cole. "Ah, yes. That was a more casual visit. I fear my unkind tone may have invited larger problems for us. I am allowed to operate here as a penance, Ellie. A punishment for abandoning a war in Faerie."

It clicked in the back of her mind. The theater show, the small hints of some great conflict and the want to escape it. "The play! It's about you? I mean, *all* of it?"

A small smile flashed across Roman's face. Gone as fast as it had appeared. "It is not a complete story, Ellie, but it is the kind of tale the humans enjoy, is it not? The Fae respond to the subtlety, and the humans to the adventure." He spread his arms wide. "The triumph of building the impossible, as it were. That is something Fae and humans alike share. But it is not the only thing, and some things are much darker."

"They're coming for an inspection?" Cole asked.

Roman inclined his head. "We have until tomorrow to be sure everyone understands what needs to be done."

"You've seen this before?" Ellie asked Cole.

"Once, yeah. It's … more annoying than anything else."

"Let us hope annoying is all we encounter tomorrow as well." Roman focused on Ellie. "As I told you, this is a punishment, and the Fae must appear miserable."

"As miserable as Bruce?" Ellie asked.

A laugh escaped Roman's lips. "Far more, I am afraid. And even the humans must be distressed."

"What do you mean by distressed? Like a coffee table?"

Roman blinked. "I do not understand, Ellie."

"Distressed wood? Like aged and kind of beat up?"

"Perhaps not so unkind as that, but certainly not happy to be working. You serve the Fae in this place, so you must be subordinate and perhaps not excited to be here."

"Well, we're screwed." Cole elbowed Ellie and grinned.

"He's serious, Cole. I'm … I'm kind of worried about this. What happens if we mess up?"

Roman gestured to her. "You understand many Fae are manipulative, Ellie, yes?"

She nodded.

"I used those methods to acquire a station here, at a gate between Faerie and the mortal world. We conceal the existence of a gate from the humans, but we also conceal the truth from the Fae who would do harm in this realm."

"The general already knows, though, right? He's been here

before."

"Yes, but he owes me a great debt, Ellie. One that cannot be repaid in a single lifetime. But he has associates who despise we who are deserters."

Ellie hesitated. "And if they find out, what happens?"

"I am not sure, but it will not be good. At minimum, a reassignment for me and those loyal to me, I suspect. They would likely dissolve our contracts and housing arrangements."

Ellie's heart hammered in her chest. "You mean I could lose my home?" Memories of time spent moving from foster home to foster home, bouncing around until she landed in a group home, until Roman finally gave her a place that *felt* like home.

Something between anger and fear slid across Roman's face, and he stepped forward, taking her hands. "You will always have a home, Ellie. I will make sure of that."

They were kind words, but it didn't stop the pressure behind her eyes, or the tears welling up in them. Cole pulled her close when Roman released her hands.

"We'll get through this, Ellie." Cole held her tight and spoke into her ear. "See, you can just cry, and they'll know you're actually miserable being here."

She laughed, but a sob escaped. The idea of losing another home ... losing another family. It was too much. It was a nightmare. Ellie pulled Cole closer.

Chapter 15

ELLIE'S ALARM BUZZED, but she was already awake. Sleep had been hard to come by, only wrapping around her in fits and starts. She rubbed her face before jumping up and hopping into a cold shower. Icy water peppered her skin for almost a minute before she finally started shivering and felt far more awake.

It was a trick, although an uncomfortable one, to get moving before the caffeine kicked in. Uniform donned and coffee in hand, Ellie left her apartment behind, a small part of her hoping it wouldn't be the last time she saw it.

She'd been assigned to ride ops on Treasure of Troll Peaks for both shifts. She figured that was to keep her out of sight of the Fae as much as possible through the night, and for that, she was grateful. The others might have been good at acting miserable when they recognized a Fae inspector coming, but Ellie wasn't sure if she could feel anything but dread for the day.

A light breeze rolled through as she made her way out of the residential area of the park and into Howling Mountain. The employee path wasn't far from the guests, and she could see the early access crowds were already lining up. Ellie pulled open a door in the mountain's side and slipped through.

She stopped by the lockers, eyed her coffee mug, and

downed the rest before stashing it away. A short walk took her backstage, where she made for the lift, finding the stairs and working her way up to the console.

"Ellie!"

She didn't stop her smile when she saw Bex. "I thought Trey was taking your shift," Ellie said.

"Not today. Are you okay?"

"I'll be alright. Just worried about tonight."

Bex dismissed the thought with a wave. "Roman knows what he's doing. We've been through these things before, though he did tell us more about Stephen this time. Did he tell you about the war in Faerie?"

"A little. Not … not much. Is it still going on?"

Bex shook her head. "Not really. A few skirmishes here and there when certain clans … how do you say it? Step over a line?"

"Like a boundary?"

"Exactly. When they come too close to another's home or territory. But there hasn't been a large battle in ten years now. Not a lot of time in Faerie, but enough that the courts will probably agree to a formal cessation soon."

"Reminds me too much of the humans, Bex."

The brownie shrugged. "We have some things in common, Ellie. I can't deny that."

Ellie winced when the lift beside her squealed and creaked. "Sounds like maintenance needs to take a look at that."

"It's scheduled for tomorrow, in fact. It's only been scream-ing since this morning. Should be fine for another shift."

Ellie relaxed into the office chair in the alcove, watching the monitors as boat after boat drifted by. In a lot of ways, she enjoyed the ride more than Kraken's Fury, but the cold from the air conditioning could get to her over a long shift.

First shift coasted by, blissfully uneventful in the dark of Treasure of Troll Peaks. The worst thing that happened was Thrud sneezed, which makes someone who's supposed to be an animatronic a little less convincing.

A few apologies at the exit, and six skip-the-line passes later, all was well.

It wasn't until Ellie and Bex had rotated out for lunch that anything cropped up. Bex had just settled into her seat when she leaned forward and squinted at the monitor.

"Is that …" She fumbled her radio. "Roman, Stephen is on the grounds. Please be aware."

A short reply came back. "Understood."

Ellie looked at the shadows in the boat. Stephen wasn't alone, but whoever was with him kept turning to static on the camera.

"What is that?" Ellie asked.

"Nothing good," Bex muttered. "Sylphs, if I had to guess. Fae of the air. They have a history with Roman. If Stephen brought them as his inspection team, no one will see them coming."

Ellie's heart sank. "So, we'll have to be extra careful tonight and act miserable."

Bex grimaced. "I'm afraid it's worse than that, Ellie. The inspectors are required to announce themselves, but they're already here. They're bending the rules."

"You mean they're already here to check on the park?"

"Yes."

Ellie stared at the monitor. "Not good, Bex. This is not

good."

THEY WATCHED IN silence until Stephen exited the ride, following on the monitors as long as they could before he was out of range. Ellie could see he turned left out of the exit.

"I'm going to follow him."

Bex rubbed at her face with both hands. "Ellie, it's too risky. I doubt he'd suspect a human of anything, but it's too risky."

"I'll look miserable and yell at Roman if I see him."

After a brief hesitation, Bex nodded. "That might actually work."

"Wish me luck." Ellie took a deep breath.

The brownie eyed her but didn't say more.

Ellie headed down the stairs to the first floor, slipping backstage and out through the northeast exit. It would give her some distance from the fairy general and hopefully give her enough space to avoid making things obvious.

She walked the border between Howling Mountain and Lost Empire, staying on the southern side of the path, where more trees gave her some semblance of cover. Ellie paused at the intersection at the central hub of the park, catching sight of Stephen in his slim, dark red button-down jacket with two translucent figures beside him. If she hadn't known what to look for, she could have mistaken them for leaves caught in a dust devil.

Ellie narrowed her eyes and cut across the bridge by Titania's Table. The occasional glance toward Carnival showed her Stephen's jacket, but when she focused on the path ahead, she saw someone else in the distance, wearing a top hat and headed into Merrows Lagoon.

Roman's pace slowed as he crossed the path where Stephen walked. *Giving him time to be seen*, Ellie thought. And sure enough, Stephen changed his direction from the theater to the central path. Roman continued into Merrows Lagoon.

There were a few ways to get into the lagoon unseen, but sometimes the simplest options were the best. Ellie stepped out behind a family with two very tall parents. She followed behind them until the path entered Merrows Lagoon and curved past the pedal boats to the Ocean Treasures.

Roman vanished behind Merrow's Feast, beyond the docks, and Stephen followed. As soon as they were all on the opposite side of the building, Ellie hurried toward the docks. She stopped when she heard voices hiding behind a beautiful wood carving of a mermaid that was nearly as tall as she was.

Ellie stood at the edge of the lagoon, listening.

"We couldn't find anything out of sorts this time, other than staff who appear well treated for those who are enduring a *punishment*, but the sylphs have filed a complaint." Ellie saw the cuff of Stephen's jacket as he gestured to the lagoon. "It is rumored you've influenced the weather in the area, and that is tantamount to encroaching on their territory."

"That is a very loose interpretation, Stephen." Roman didn't sound angry. He sounded calm, almost defeated. And Ellie suspected that was exactly the point.

The leaves and whirlwind beside Stephen spoke. "It is ours and ours alone, Roman. Your transgressions will not go unpunished."

Stephen continued before Roman could so much as respond. "You're due in the courts. I am to inform you the gate to

Faerie has been shut."

Roman removed his top hat and ran his fingernails along the brim as he stepped into view. "And how would you suggest I reach the courts without the gate?"

"Find another gate. It is no concern of ours."

Ellie waited for Roman to snap at Stephen, talk him down, something, but Roman only nodded.

"Then I will see you in Faerie in the morning."

Stephen hesitated. "That would be quite a sight." The general said no more as he walked away, headed for the front gates of the park, two windy figures hovering beside him.

Ellie tucked herself into a ball behind the carved mermaid as they passed, edging toward the back until they were out of view.

"Boss, what are you going to do?" Mateo asked.

Ellie gasped as the gators stood up out of the lagoon just across from her. She hadn't seen the merest hint of them there.

Roman leaned around the corner and raised an eyebrow. "It would seem I need to pay better attention to my meeting places to start." He gestured for all three of them to come closer. "Cole, would you join us?"

Ellie stared as Cole stood up from behind a low bush, a sheepish grin on his face. "I ... was curious."

"Mateo, Valentina, is the nearest gate still in Florida?" The air shimmered as Roman sent some small magic into the world, likely obscuring the view from any prying eyes.

The two gators looked at each other before Valentina answered. "As far as we know, it's still in the lake near Orlando."

"That doesn't narrow it down," Ellie whispered.

Roman smiled briefly. "Would you both be comfortable

accompanying me?"

Mateo rubbed his claws together. "Might we wear a concealment charm? I would prefer not to travel in the cargo hold like last time."

"Quite cold." Valentina agreed.

"Yes. First class, so there will be plenty of room and you will not draw attention." He paused. "Much attention. In exchange, you will escort me to the gate."

"Agreed," the gators said in unison.

"You're going to fly to Florida?" Ellie asked. "With two gators? In first class?"

"Yes."

"Okay."

"I will give the details to Capy. This is not a meeting I can forsake. I will return tomorrow by midnight. Ellie and Cole will act with authority in my absence. Any issues or needs that arise, they will be consulted as if owners themselves. Should anything happen that prevents my return to the realm, they will be the new owners in full."

"A wise choice," Mateo said with a nod.

Ellie stared at Roman. "What? Why wouldn't you come back? Why would, what?"

"I will be in touch, Ellie. Through whatever trials await, you will have news of what transpires in Faerie." He turned to Cole. "Watch over them all, Cole. As you would your family."

"I … I will." Cole tilted his head back, his eyes determined.

"Mateo, Valentina, with me. We will visit HR to acquire the necessary concealment charms, and journey forth."

That was the last time Ellie saw Roman before he departed for Faerie.

ELLIE SAT WITH Cole in HR, trying to understand, even though Capy had just explained the entire situation.

"What do you *mean*?"

Gus threw his paws up in the air, but Capy, ever patient, went over every detail one more time.

"The park is yours, should anything befall Roman. It is as simple as that, Ellie. He trusts you, and he knows many of the Fae, no matter how benevolent, will not understand the needs of the humans as well as you and Cole."

Ellie rubbed hard at her forehead. "That's insane, Capy. But he'll be okay, right?"

"He is resourceful. The judgment handed down by the Faerie court will not take long. Two days, perhaps less, if all goes well."

Cole leaned forward in his chair beside Ellie. "And how often does all go well?"

Capy's nose twitched.

"Right," Cole muttered.

Gus sighed and swiped a paw across his phone. "Roman thought you might enjoy this." He turned the screen to Ellie and Cole, revealing Roman in a way she'd never seen, adorned in sunglasses, cargo pants, and a loud, yellow Hawaiian shirt. He stood beside two mountain-sized humans.

"Roman and the gators?" Cole asked.

Ellie did a double take. "The two who look like they could win a strongman tournament are the *gators*?"

Gus tapped on the larger of the two, holding an older DSLR camera. "That's Mateo." He zoomed in. "You can just make out the concealment charm around his neck." Gus zipped across the photo, pointing out Valentina's wide straw hat, beach bag, and Crocs.

Ellie blinked. "Crocs? Are you serious?"

Capy let out a low laugh. "She thought the name was funny. I do not believe she has any idea how polarizing they are among the humans."

Gus flipped over to Roman.

"Is that a Ninja Turtle shirt?" Cole asked, squinting.

Gus nodded and zoomed in on the finely tailored button-down, Ninja Turtles plastered all over it in repeating patterns on a bright yellow background. "I thought the knock-off sunglasses were a nice touch, myself. They'll certainly make it through the airport undetected."

"Send me that," Ellie said. "I want to keep it forever and torment Roman with it."

Gus's claws clicked on the screen. "Done."

"You two best get ready for the evening shift. The park is going to need you."

Ellie glanced at the clock on the wall. "Three hours. We can get some food, get changed, and try to prepare for being leads."

"Owners," Capy corrected.

Cole shook his head. "No, Roman will be back. You'll see. We'll help tonight, and then he'll be back."

"I do hope that's the case." Capy offered a small smile.

AFTER DINNER AND milkshakes at the bar in Titania's Table, a quick shower, and a change of clothes, Ellie and Cole were ready to face the evening shift. In short order, Ellie understood how busy Roman stayed during a day at the Theme Park at the End of the World.

The first call on her radio was for an angry Fae at the front gate who had apparently misunderstood the ticket packages online. It happened sometimes with the less technically inclined Fae, but Ellie had spent enough time with Capy to know how to defuse a tense situation.

She reached guest services by the park's gate within a minute of the call coming through. Instead of stepping inside the booth to further draw a line between her and the guests, she stayed outside to stand next to them. A family of great porcupines, which were intimidating, to say the least.

"Hi! I'm Ellie." She sounded perkier than she felt. "I understand you're having an issue with your ticket package?"

"A manager, finally. This … *employee*." The great porcupine waved at Trey, standing on the counter behind the window as the quills on her back bristled. "This brownie tells me my child isn't included in our family package because he's just over 500 years old. That is *ridiculous*."

The brownie, much to his credit, didn't look angry. If Ellie hadn't known Trey, she might not have caught the rigid tension in his back as he denied the porcupine family entrance.

"I am sorry, my lady, but that has been the park policy for the past five years. Anyone 250 years or older, even accompanied by an adult, must have a ticket. It helps us keep the park safe and staffed for the crowds. We can't have everyone dropping their kids off without being compensated. Especially during *human* hours."

The porcupine looked at Ellie with something like surprise. "You jest about your own kind?"

"Oh, yes. I much prefer the company of Fae, my lady. I know it's an inconvenience and an unwelcome surprise to need another ticket. Could I compensate you with complimentary skip-the-line passes? They'll be good once at each ride and will save you quite a lot of time."

The great porcupine slowly tilted her head to the side. "Well, yes, that would be most generous."

Ellie pulled a gold-foil ticket out of her pocket. "And for the little one. A free snack at whatever stand you like. Or, if you brave Titania's Table, they have a delightful cut comb milkshake this evening."

She turned her attention to Trey. "Go ahead and comp those skip-the-lines when they purchase the last ticket, Trey."

"Already set it up, Ellie."

"Good, thanks for the help." She turned to the family again. "And you all please have a wonderful night in the Theme Park at the End of the World." She offered a short bow before walking away, taking a great deal of satisfaction from the stunned look on the great porcupine's face as her quills settled along her back.

The night progressed, and she spoke with Cole on the radio more than actually seeing him in person. From one land to the next, they made emergency runs to refill ingredients at the corn dog stands, address guest satisfaction issues, and cover breaks where rides were shorthanded for the night.

They were in the last two hours of the park being open when Ellie's radio squawked. She turned the volume up when she missed the first words as she walked by Puffing Demons.

Bex's panicked voice came across in staticky bursts. "Code gray! Code gray at Troll Peaks!"

"No. No no no." Ellie sprinted through Lost Empire, boots hammering the stone as she headed straight for Howling Mountain. Code gray meant a piece of human technology had malfunctioned. There was only so much the Fae could do when it came to some of the iron-rich metals. "Cole, get to Howling Mountain. Now!"

"Almost there."

Ellie hurdled the shrubs blocking the path to the north employee entrance, clicking her radio again. "Bex, where?"

"The lift! Ellie, hurry! The boat!"

Her eyes didn't have time to adjust in the pitch-black of backstage. Ellie navigated by the lights on the floor alone, memory taking her down the right paths that led to the lift until the lights clicked on, and she stopped dead in her tracks.

The belt had ripped, spinning one of the boats to the side, the impact knocking a guard rail loose. A boatful of Fae kids screamed, getting far more than they'd bargained for with the churning rollers of steel and iron just below them.

One of them tried to stand.

"Stay seated!" Ellie yelled as loud as she could. "Bex, stop the lift!"

"It won't stop, Ellie!" Panic tore through Bex's voice.

If the Fae fell into those rollers, they didn't have a chance of surviving. "Cut the power!"

"We did! We took it off the generator!"

Only then did Ellie understand what had happened. The ride didn't break down. The guardrail hadn't simply come away with the impact. They'd been sabotaged. That was likely why Stephen had come earlier than expected to draw Roman away.

"I can save them."

Ellie spun and found Cole standing close by. "How? Tell me how!"

"I'm not … I'm not like you, Ellie. I don't want to scare you. I'm … like them."

She couldn't understand what he was saying. Like who? The Fae? And everything came crashing together in her mind. Cole wasn't the only other human in the park. Cole had never *been* human. She reached out and grabbed his arm. "I don't care what you are, Cole. You're my family and I love you."

Cole's eyes widened. There was a moment of hesitation. And then he wasn't Cole anymore. His skin grayed, his body thinning as whipcord muscles stood out along his arms, and his pants grew just a little too short.

The boat wrenched to the side, teetering on the edge.

"Save them!"

Cole leapt. Not onto the belt, but into the rollers themselves.

"Cole, no!" Ellie watched in horror as he slammed into the iron and steel, raising a hand before plunging it into the gears of the rollers. Smoke and screeching metal spewed into the air as the kids screamed.

With one foot, Cole lashed out, denting a roller and leaping forward, catching the edge of the boat before dragging it back onto the track. The entire top of the lift stilled. The base smoked, and after another few seconds, ground to a halt.

"With me, with me now." Cole gathered three kids up in his left arm and leapt to the walkway before going back for the last two. "You're okay now. You're okay."

The smallest of them, a young slibreg, wailed at the top of his lungs. "That was so much scarier than Mom said it was!"

Bex stood on the walkway, ushering the kids forward through the emergency paths. Another brownie caught them at the intersection and offered to walk them out. Bex only nodded, wordless.

She turned back with tears in her eyes. "I thought we lost them. I couldn't carry them. I just ... and now Cole. You shouldn't have had to do that! Reveal yourself like ..." A sob escaped her lips.

Cole glanced at Ellie, taller now, and thinner, his eyes a midnight black. But it was still Cole. It was still his eyes and his hands that had saved those lives. Ellie reached out to him, but he pulled away.

"Ellie, I can't. I didn't want you to know. I didn't ..." he turned and rushed down the walkway, disappearing out of the emergency lights and going backstage.

"Give him time, Ellie," Bex said after a sniff. "I feel so bad for him."

Everything in her screamed to follow, but she didn't know if she'd make everything worse. She had so many questions, so many things she wanted to say, and none of them felt like enough.

Chapter 16

SHE DIDN'T SEE Cole again the rest of the night, but she heard his voice on the radio. He was still helping with the shift, but it hurt Ellie's heart how he managed to avoid her. Even after the park closed, she didn't feel like sleeping, instead staying after to help with third shift.

No one mentioned Cole, as if they either didn't know, or everyone had always known except her. A Fae! And she didn't even know what kind of Fae. She'd never seen anything like him before. And how rude would that be to ask? She could only imagine it would be one of the rudest things in the world.

Ellie worked through most of the shift, spending a good amount of time with Thrud and Yngvarr in the center of Treasure of Troll Peaks. With the walls pushed backstage, they could reach the lift to study it, though neither touched the metal without gloves. And troll gloves were quite a sight.

Thrud held the belt and turned it over. "It's clearly been cut. I'm afraid you were correct, Ellie. This was sabotage.

"And this was not broken at the weld. It was cut nearly through by the finest of blades." Yngvarr gestured to the railing.

Ellie closed her eyes for a moment while she sat on the walkway beside them. "Why? What does Stephen get out of it?"

"I suspect Stephen owes a debt to someone else, Ellie,"

Yngvarr said, his voice booming through the cavernous space. "And if it was sylphs you saw, I'd wager a good portion of my horde on them holding that debt."

"How do we keep it from happening again? A sabotage like that?"

Thrud glanced at Yngvarr. "The simplest solution would be to ban *all* weapons within this place. Even those of the Fae."

Ellie blinked. "You mean they aren't already?"

"No. That would be considered a slight by many."

Ellie stood up. "Well, a human wouldn't know that, would she?"

A wide smile crossed Thrud's lips. "No, I suspect not."

"As I'm acting owner until Roman gets back, I have a new rule to put in place. Is Wendy usually in the office this late?"

Yngvarr nodded. "We often see her leaving when we visit the kraken in Merrows Lagoon to share a barrel of mead. She'll likely be there another hour."

Ellie turned the frequency on her radio and clicked the button. "Wendy, are you in the office still? I need to speak with you."

As soon as Wendy confirmed she was, Ellie took off, heading across the park.

ELLIE SAT IN the corner of Wendy's large cubicle, waiting for her to respond. Wendy's trunk sifted through a stack of papers while her toes worked an enormous keyboard.

"There isn't an established protocol for anything like this, Ellie. And you must understand, even if we enforced the weapons ban during Fae hours that we have for human hours, it won't negate the magic many Fae wield."

"It would have stopped Stephen and the sylphs, wouldn't it?"

"A binding agreement?" Wendy's typing slowed and her trunk reached over to the mouse, zooming in on one particular article. "It would have, Ellie. Yes, they could not have cut through steel without it." She frowned at the screen and glanced up at Ellie.

"These are the original oaths the park was founded on. Roman gave you the authority of an owner in full, Ellie. We can do this, if you wish."

"Yes. Can we have it ready by tomorrow?"

Wendy inclined her head. "We can, but many tickets were purchased under the existing rules, and such agreements cannot be altered with the Fae. At least, not without putting us at a serious disadvantage."

Ellie tapped her chin before biting her lips. "Then we let Bruce loose."

"Excuse me?" Wendy sat up straighter.

"He's always wanted more help in security. Let's give it to him. He can post more staff backstage to keep an eye on things. We'll have to pay more overtime, but it's worth it. Temporarily, until the new tickets are the only ones in circulation. Oh! And we could offer free skip-the-line tickets to anyone who trades the old tickets in."

Wendy tapped her trunk on the desk. "That is devious, Ellie." She paused for a moment before offering a sly smile. "Roman would be proud. I'll get things arranged with Bruce. *You* go get some rest. You and Cole did a good job tonight."

"I still haven't seen him." She balled her fist.

Wendy pulled away from her computer. "Ellie, give him time. He's a young Fae who has had a secret revealed before he was ready. Cole will heal in time."

"How bad was he hurt?"

"I meant his heart will heal, Ellie. The wounds from the iron are superficial. Much like grabbing a freshly microwaved egg and having it explode."

Ellie blinked at that. "That's … really specific. You have a story there, Wendy?"

The elephant harrumphed.

REST CAME FAR easier than Ellie expected. She woke up to a small puddle of drool on her pillow and hair that had a mind of its own. She supposed it was like that sometimes, sheer exhaustion winning out over the stress and worry for Cole.

A quick shower while a new pot of coffee brewed had her feeling a little more like facing whatever the day might bring. She rubbed the fuzzy head of a pooka plush Cole had won for her several months ago. She hoped he wouldn't be avoiding her again.

Ellie started into the park, wanting to grab more of a breakfast than the toaster pastries she had stashed in her apartment. Grocery shopping had been on the schedule, but Roman's departure sent everything into chaos.

"Ellie! Ellie!"

She turned to find Franzi waving at her from the window of Nordic Eats.

"Hi, Franzi."

"I just wanted to tell you I heard about the new park policies." Franzi clasped her paws together. "We're so happy about it, Ellie. I just can't even tell you."

"Wendy already told everyone?" Ellie blinked.

"Word travels fast in the park. I didn't mean to keep you from your morning!"

She smiled at Franzi and continued on, looping past Titania's Table on her way into the Dark Forest. She texted Cole as she crossed into the land.

Ellie: *Breakfast?*

Cole: *Just waiting for you.*

His response had come fast, and a terrible knot of dread worked to untie itself in her gut. Ellie's pace quickened, and soon enough she was past the cobra roll of Gowrow's Cave, and headed toward the café behind HR.

She spotted Cole in the corner of the room and waved when he glanced up. He looked different than he had the night before, his eyes back to their crystal blue and gray color, the same face she was used to seeing every day.

He returned her wave, then went back to watching something on his phone.

Ellie took a deep breath and headed over to the chafing dishes, curious what would be on the buffet that morning. French toast came first, then a creamy dish of scrambled eggs topped with fresh green onion. The only thing missing was her favorite hot sauce, and almost as soon as she thought it, she saw the bottles of Cholula at the end of the counter.

Hot sauce and syrup in hand, Ellie made her way to Cole's table.

"Good morning?"

"Hi," Cole said, only stealing a glance before focusing on the phone again.

"Did you get some sleep?"

He shook his head. "Not a lot. You know, things like that take it out of me."

Ellie wasn't sure if he meant the change, or the worry. "Is your hand okay?"

He held it up and turned it as if that was an answer. It might have looked normal, but how could she be sure? Could she even ask without offending him? Instead of being too forward, Ellie scooted her chair closer.

Cole swiveled the phone so she could see better, too. "Looks like the Taters finally got that corn dog episode edited. They left you in the background a couple times." A brief smile crossed his lips.

"Really?" She leaned closer, taking a bite of egg.

Cole swiped back a bit and paused the screen. Sure enough, there was Ellie with her mouth distended with a corned beef corn dog.

She groaned.

"It's not so bad."

They watched in silence for a time, laughing at Poe's terrible jokes and Tottie's ability to take larger bites than any human should be able to while speaking clearly. Ellie worked her way through the eggs and French toast, knowing she should have been gushing about them, but Cole still wasn't saying much.

He checked the time when the video wound down. "I think I'd better get to work. I'll see you later."

It was almost a question, and it broke Ellie's heart. She

reached out and squeezed his arm as he walked away.

She jumped when a tray crashed down next to her a moment later and Capy wiggled into the seat beside her, wearing a carefully ironed blue vest.

"Capy?"

A smaller tray clattered onto the table, spilling a cup of nuts. Gus chittered at the nuts and then flopped into the smaller seat beside Capy.

"Gus?"

"You looked like you could use some company," Capy said. "And perhaps, some welcome news?"

"Please, yes."

Gus cracked into a nut and gestured to Ellie. "And maybe see how you're doing now that you know Cole's a changeling."

"A changeling?" Ellie asked. The stories she'd heard about changelings were terrifying. Invading families, stealing kids. But that couldn't be Cole. "Why didn't anyone tell me?"

"Well, it's not like he's a weregoose, is it?" Gus gestured toward the door. "Imagine that. Cole with a temper like Bruce?" The squirrel whistled. "No, thank you."

"Bruce is a ... weregoose?" Ellie's forehead bunched up as she tried to wrap her head around that, and also tried figure out what a weregoose was. "Does he have feathers?"

Capy nodded. "Once a year, when the weather changes."

"What is my life?" Ellie groaned. "But Cole's a changeling? Did he ... did he steal someone?"

"Cole?" Gus blurted out. "Not likely. He—"

Capy gave Gus a stern look. "It is not your story to tell, Gus."

Gus flicked a walnut shell away and puffed out a breath.

"Fine, fine. Just leave Ellie to stress over it then. That's much better. What next? You're going to tell her about the human legs booth?"

Capy's eyes grew as wide as saucers. "Gus, no."

"Human legs booth?" Ellie asked, not quite keeping the apprehension out of her question.

"It was only an idea. It never happened." Capy pointed at Gus. "A terrible misunderstanding."

Gus chomped down on another nut. "Like turkey legs! Humans love turkey legs."

"Is that why Roman told me to stay away from the barbecue after hours?" Ellie asked, horrified.

Capy shook her head and released a kind of barking chuckle. "No, Ellie, no. That was because of the magic. A little too strong for the human palate."

"Like the churros?" Ellie asked.

"I heard about that." Gus picked up a cashew. "Are you doing okay, though, Ellie?"

When she didn't answer, Capy spoke. "Perhaps our other news would help?"

Gus frowned. "Oh, you mean Roman's coming back today? Or the fact he's standing behind her right now?"

Ellie's heart hammered in her chest. She turned to find Roman waiting behind her, back in his black jacket and top hat. She almost leapt out of her seat, hurrying to give him a hug.

"I'm so glad you're back. Roman, I was so worried."

"I appreciate your concern, Ellie. All is well. Better than that, in fact. The courts have signed the treaty to end the War of Realms. There is no need to hide ourselves from their inspectors any longer." He patted her on the back.

"It's over?" Gus asked. "Truly over?"

"There are still loyalists, Gus, but yes, it is over." Roman inclined his head.

Ellie pulled him closer before letting go. "Did they tell you what happened here? With Cole and … and everything?"

"Yes, Ellie. I wish Cole could have told you in his own time. He always meant to, but he feared what may come of it."

"Why?"

Roman glanced away. "You know enough of the Fae to know what changelings are, Ellie. You understand what they have done in the past."

"But Cole?"

"It is not my place to tell that story. Not without his blessing. I will say he has never harmed a child. No matter what direction he was given." Roman met her eyes. "You must understand that changelings are happier living out their lies. It is their natural state."

Cole stepped back into view behind Roman. His skin had a gray pallor to it again, his eyes black as a desert night. But they were still his.

Ellie held her hand out and Cole came forward, reaching out to take it as his gaze flicked between her and Roman.

"Did you enchant her?" Cole asked.

"No."

"Enchant me?" Ellie's voice rose with the question. "What do you mean?"

Roman clasped his hands together. "I would never do anything without your permission, Ellie, but I *could* remove the memory, if you wish. Everything can be as it was." He waved his hand and Cole was back to his human form, the same as if nothing had ever changed. "You would only remember his guise."

She squeezed Cole's hand harder. "No, Roman. We don't forget our friends."

Cole shook, almost hurting her hand he squeezed it so hard. It was all the warning Ellie had before he scooped her up in a crushing hug. There was no changeling in that moment, no human, only a love for each other that would weather any storm.

Chapter 17

"I ALWAYS THOUGHT I'd need to go to a tattoo parlor," Ellie said.

"Wouldn't you need a guardian to sign a waiver or something for that?" Cole asked, sitting at the end of the bar at Titania's Table while Ellie had her arm stretched across it.

"I would gladly give it." Roman ran a finger from her elbow to her wrist, adjusting the angle of his grip as he went before making two marks with an ancient green pen. "Ellie has a good head on her shoulders, as the humans say."

"I could get a capybara tattoo on my shoulder!" Ellie nodded. "That's a great idea."

"That is not what I said." Roman raised an eyebrow. "Now, hold still. We do not want to repeat the churro incident."

Roman's forehead creased as he focused, holding Ellie motionless with an iron grip. His eyes closed briefly before he muttered something she didn't understand. Roman laid his fingers closer to her wrist, his eyes unfocused as he whispered more.

Ellie felt a spike of cold, and then nothing.

"It does not have the same painful recovery as a human tattoo, but it is no less permanent."

She looked down at her arm, a perfect shield knot gracing it, the ink almost glittering when she moved. Below that was something else, an oblong knot that formed a right angle, and at its peak sat a simple triquetra in the center.

"The shield knot you have always wanted, Ellie. And a gift. Without exchange. There is no name in the human tongue for this."

Cole hopped up to look at Roman's work. "It kind of looks like two sailors knots with a triquetra in the middle."

Roman looked at him in horror. "I think not. Look at the angles. The … the … no. Cole, *no*."

Ellie grinned at Cole. It was a rare day when someone flustered Roman. She turned her attention back to the older Fae. "Thank you, Roman. Thank you so much. Is it ready? I mean, can I try it tonight?"

"You can, indeed. No ride is off-limits for you now, in whatever form it takes."

"How long do we have?" Ellie asked Cole.

Cole leaned forward, his lips curling up. "Thirty minutes until we're open for Fae hours. The humans are already out. Tinker's Escape?"

"Tinker's Escape!"

Ellie hopped off the stool and hesitated. "Thank you, Roman. Truly."

"You offer thanks too easily, Ellie."

"I don't think I do. I learned from a wise old Fae."

Roman smiled and dismissed them with a wave. "Go. Enjoy the night. You both deserve this."

ELLIE DIDN'T LET go of Cole's hand as they made their way through the park. Some of the hesitation had left him. She could feel his warmth again, how he leaned toward her as he spoke, but there were times he looked away, his jaw flexing.

"What is it, Cole? If something's wrong, you can tell me. Just know that."

He gave her a small smile. It wasn't bright or cheery, but it was Cole. "No, Ellie. This is a good day, and I don't want to burden you with simple things."

"Tell me." Ellie squeezed his hand again.

"It's silly. Honestly, it's just …" Cole gestured to himself, his slightly taller, grayer self. "I can look like you remember me if you want. I'll need to for the human hours anyway, and if you're more comfortable, you know. I can do that all the time."

Ellie stopped and waited for Cole to meet her eyes. "However you're comfortable, Cole. However you're *you*." She pushed herself up on her toes and kissed his cheek, sinking into him as he wrapped his arms around her.

"Thank you, Ellie."

She didn't miss the small crack in his voice and didn't let go until he did.

Cole took a deep breath and squeezed her hand again. "Well, you ready to ride?"

Ellie doubted it was possible to grin any wider.

They took off into Lost Empire, almost at a jog, but still slow enough Bruce wouldn't yell at them if he was nearby.

For the first time in a long time, Ellie didn't stop to study the details in the queue or listen so hard to the soundscaping she could pick out every noise. Instead, she rubbed her hands together as they entered the station, a confused-looking Kevin on the other side of the tracks.

"Hey, you two, what are you doing here?" His eyebrows

rose ever higher.

"I'm here to ride," Ellie said with a wicked grin.

"Umm. We're already set for Fae hours, Ellie. It'll have to wait until the morning."

She held her arm up, brandished with the glittering shield knot and Roman's triquetra.

Kevin blinked. "Roman did it? I mean, you can, oh this is amazing, do you have any idea Ellie … I mean no human has ever …" He ran his fingers through his hair and signaled to the other ride ops. "Give me five minutes. Let's get this train ready!"

Ellie laughed when Kevin raised his radio and sent a general call out. "I need volunteers to ride Tinker's Escape with our first human! You have four minutes to get here." Kevin pointed to the front row. "You two, get in there."

By the time ride ops lined up down either side of the platform to check restraints, the entire train was full. Ellie gripped the restraints, nerves flipping her stomach with excitement as Kevin finally disappeared into the preshow area. Ellie thought he might be just as excited as her and Cole. If not more.

"Why did I agree to this?"

Ellie turned and grinned at Capy in the row behind them. "Because you love me."

"Bro!" Manfred shouted from near the back of the train. "No, because this is iconic, bro! History bro!"

Bex and Trey waved from the last car and Ellie almost bounced in her seat. Even two of the mermaids had joined them, Shay and another, traversing the queue in their wheelchairs before transferring.

The seat beside Capy was empty. Ellie wasn't sure why until

Roman slid into it.

"You're riding with us?" Ellie clapped her hands.

"Obviously." His voice was even and reserved as always.

Ride ops began their check, making sure each lap bar was properly secured. Ellie saw the thumbs up and didn't quite believe it as the train rolled forward to the preshow.

The sliding door vibrated like any other time. The boom drowned out every other noise in that space until Kevin ran onstage in his full tinker regalia.

"You all made it this far! Can you hear them? The guards are getting close now. Try to get our human out alive." He winked at Ellie. "Keep your hands and anything else you'd like to keep attached inside the vehicle. Hands up. Head back. Bars down. Hold on to your butts." And then Ellie heard the line reserved for the Fae hours. "Take the underground passage!"

The room spun, faster than she'd realized when she'd been standing on the walkway. The track tilted down as it slid along the curve, until they were held at 90 degrees, staring straight into nothing, all their weight against the lap bar. A motor hummed, and the train shot forward.

Ellie screamed. An unbridled joy as the force of the launch tried to pulverize her in her seat before the first turn threatened to crack bones with the lateral force. The small fires during the human hours had been replaced with infernos, searing heat from towering flames lighting the spaghetti bowl the second before they hit it.

Her arm warmed beneath the protection Roman had given her as she endured a tangle of track twice as long as the human version, another launch set into the middle of it all. Ellie's vision dimmed with the last helix as they fired out of the spaghetti bowl.

Capy screeched behind her, and Ellie put her arms in the air, bracing against the front of the train with her feet. Cole joined her as they launched into the next tunnel, the guards and halberds still there from the human hours, but somehow more menacing, darker. Ellie loved every second of it.

The third launch hit, and it was as if Ellie had never experienced a coaster launch in her life. The force pinned her arms back over her head and she howled with the rest of the train. Even Roman's baritone shout could be heard over the roar of the wind and metal.

They soared up the side of the top hat, taking it at a speed that should have torn the top off it before plunging down the drop. Her vision grayed again at the sudden turn following it before the track inverted, hanging them in a zero-G stall for the blink of an eye. It was the only element Ellie thought might be more intense in the daytime because the riders were suspended longer.

All thoughts left her in the helix, the crushing weight of it pushing her arms back down into her lap no matter how hard she tried to raise them. The airtime hill in the middle felt like it was trying to throw her into the darkness, and it was wonderful.

"Here we go!" Cole shouted, bracing himself as the heartline roll came into view.

Even Ellie, who almost never held on for any roller coaster, had a death grip on her restraint. They hit the roll, and it tried its best to throw them all into the deeps. It was over so fast, it felt as though the track was still twisting around them. And then she saw the second roll.

Cole's shriek could have been soundscaping. It was the same as every other time Ellie had ridden Tinker's Escape with him.

Ellie laughed and grinned as they rolled. The lap bar caught against their thighs and kept them from a terrible fall before they were upright again, being forced into the bottom of their seats once more.

The following turns put them into the final tunnel, slamming them into the brake run in front of the animatronic knight and his giant jumping spider. He gestured with his halberd in the mountain cavern.

"You made it, tinkers! Well done. Don't forget to retrieve your loose articles from the lockers. For the Steamsworn!"

They rolled back into the station. Kevin waited with the largest smile she'd ever seen on him. "Let's hear it for our human! She survived."

Ellie jerked back in her seat when the entire station roared, and she found half the park staff standing in the queue. She couldn't stop the flood of warmth in her chest, or the tears on her cheek. There was nothing like seeing family so happy for you.

Roman let out an exasperated breath. "I believe I need a churro."

Ellie leaned over and grabbed Cole in a hug as soon as the restraints opened. "That was amazing, Cole. I can't believe it. I didn't think I'd recognize so many elements, you know? But then some of them were *so* different. I can't even describe it."

Cole patted his chest when she released him. "I haven't ridden it at night in so long. I'd almost forgotten how insane that is!"

Kevin stepped closer on the platform. "Ellie, if you're up for it, there are a few other team members who would like to ride with you."

She glanced at Cole and grinned. "Yes!"

Chapter 18

S UMMER ENDED AND Corn Dog Crave Days left with it. Ellie thought the Taters might have been sadder about that than anyone else. She loved the corn dogs, but not as much as the Taters did by the end of the season. In fact, their *prolific* number of episodes covering the corn dogs in detail had made it hard to keep the ingredients stocked for the Korean corn dog and the grillpølse, as two of their shorts had gone viral. Far more guests than expected had come to the parks because of it.

Fall brought a vibrant palette of reds and yellows and browns to the hills all around the Theme Park at the End of the World. It looked like a different place as the seasons changed. It wouldn't be long before the coldest months came, sometimes shutting down the park due to ice and frigid temperatures.

Cold wouldn't stop the Fae hours, of course. Roman always saw to that.

It had been a week since basic construction started on the haunted houses for Halloween. Ellie couldn't wait for that, though they still had time before the real chaos began. The Fae could have done it faster but keeping human suspicions at bay was always a priority for Roman.

Ellie stopped by the pretzel stand on her way to the Bobsled roller coaster. She leaned on the counter and waved to Hans. "Morning!"

"Hi, Ellie. Pepperoni this morning? We have a pumpkin spice pretzel we're working on if you'd like to try it."

"Maybe later? I *need* that pepperoni."

His whiskers twitched with amusement as he grabbed a parchment paper bag and stuffed a pretzel in it from the warmer. "Fresh batch this morning. Roman likes his churros, and you like your pretzels."

"Nothing wrong with that." Ellie grinned and took the offered pretzel.

She wandered by the games in Carnival, passing Whimsy Carousel as she made her way to the central hub. It was the long way to get to the Bobsled, but she was early, and she certainly didn't want the pretzel to get cold.

She was halfway through that glorious twist of mozzarella and pepperoni, grease threatening to drip onto her work clothes before she froze. A familiar face walked by in a hat pulled low over his head.

Ellie dropped the pretzel into its parchment bag and raised her radio, her words barely above a whisper. "Roman. Stephen's in the park. I swear it's him. Cardinals hat and a leathery-looking windbreaker. Walking toward Howling Mountain."

"What is a Cardinals hat?" Roman asked.

"Baseball team? Red hat? Bird on it?"

"Ah, yes. Thank you, Ellie. I am on my way."

She followed Stephen at a distance, munching on her pretzel as she waited for Roman. Ellie frowned when Stephen turned into Howling Mountain, headed for the walkway that would take him to Treasure of Troll Peaks.

Security had only recently drawn back to near-normal levels, but Ellie knew Bruce had a guard stationed by every ride that involved older human technology. It might not have been impossible to sabotage some of the magic in other parts of the park, but it would certainly be harder than the machinery. And the sabotage from the last time Stephen had been there had taken almost two weeks to repair.

Roman's top hat caught the light, drawing attention near the entrance to the apartments as he strode forward, angling for Stephen.

Ellie wasn't sure what to think of the general's presence in the park. He'd taken enough care to disguise himself among the humans. Certainly more care than the last time, when he'd shown up with sylphs in tow.

"Stephen," Roman called as he reached the intersection of walkways between backstage and the path to the queue.

Ellie didn't miss Stephen's clenched fists.

He stopped and glared at Roman. "Is this not a public place?"

"Yes. All are welcome here, until they are banned for sabotage."

"I was not formally notified of that." Stephen gestured widely to the park. "Is there no room here for old allies?"

Roman tilted his head to the side, ever so slightly. "Understand, Stephen, the rules of my exile here for the war kept me from responding adequately when you brought a saboteur into my home. That is no longer a factor."

"And you still harbor that girl here." He pointed at Ellie without turning, as though he'd known exactly where she was the entire time. Stephen didn't break eye contact with Roman. Didn't so much as blink. "The sylphs acted without my knowledge."

Roman slowly crossed his arms. "Indeed. Your knowledge of what, I suppose, is the question. Bruce, please escort Stephen from the park."

Ellie looked around, not seeing a sign of the security guard before a massive white goose suddenly stormed out of the bushes, wings raised and honking like a freight train as he charged Stephen.

"Bruce has impulse control issues in this state," Roman called out as Stephen backpedaled. "You might want to run."

"Go get him, Bruce!" Cole called as he hurdled the bushes behind the goose, wearing a security badge of his own.

"You're mad!" Stephen shouted over his shoulder. "You abandoned your post! Corrupted your clans, and for that, there *will* be consequences."

"Do as you must."

Stephen wheeled around and drew a slender length of wood from his jacket.

Roman flinched.

"Roman?" Ellie hissed.

"Ellie!" Cole shouted as he lunged forward.

The strike came fast. Stephen spun on Ellie. A flash of violent blue sparked from the wood and slipped past Bruce's raised wings. The goose turned, running for Ellie, but he was far too slow. The spell slammed into her chest before funneling down her arm, her tattoo burning like the coals of a great fire. She threw her hand forward through instinct alone, trying to keep the blue flame as far away as she could. Then it was gone, arcing through the air, crashing into the same wood Stephen had attacked her with, consuming it in an instant.

There was only silence in that place, and the tiniest hint of an annoyed smile on Roman's lips.

"You are a *traitor*, Roman! A human! This transgression will—"

"Leave my home. The treaty has been signed. The war is done. We are unbound by the old ways."

"That human must perish. She is a stain on the power of Faerie! It is enough you harbor a changeling with no prize. It is enough we allow him to live."

Ellie glanced at Cole. He stood tall at Roman's side, not flinching at Stephen's words. His changeling form on full display.

"Humans deserve more than tragedy. Go home and be with Isabelle, Stephen. I will not ask again."

Stephen stepped forward, and Bruce roared, wheeling back around to attack. There was no hesitation as Bruce pounced, the first strike of his beak drawing blood from Stephen's forehead. The brush of a great wing slammed him to the ground. It was finally enough to get the message through. Stephen ran.

Bruce followed, and Ellie could still hear the honking of the weregoose as he chased Stephen through the park's gates.

Roman frowned at the retreating chaos. "Let us hope he abandons this. His wife, Isabelle, has fought against this conflict for ages."

"Ellie, are you okay?" Cole slipped behind Roman, coming over to her.

"I am, yeah." She ran her fingers over the tattoo Roman had given her. "What is this?"

"A protection rarely given to humans, Ellie. Some would

call it a blessing of the Fae. It will not protect you from all magic, but some of the more hostile spells—those meant for war and nothing more—will find no purchase."

Ellie reached out and took Cole's hand as Bruce waddled back down the path. Angry hisses and honks echoed out from the goose's bill, and Ellie couldn't help but smile.

"Thank you, Bruce."

The goose honked again.

"Do you like pretzels?" Ellie glanced at Roman. "Can he eat pretzels like this? Or is he like a real goose?"

The last third of her pretzel vanished as Bruce lunged for it, shaking his head back and forth before tilting it back and gobbling the pretzel down. He let out a low honk and waddled back into the bushes.

"Both," Roman said.

Chapter 19

IT WAS ONLY a day before the first big storm of the season rolled in. Thunderclouds and lightning delayed all the outdoor rides an hour before the lunch rush, which meant the restaurants, games, and indoor attractions would be packed until the front passed.

Ellie watched from the pub on Dublin Street, snacking on a basket of fish and chips soaked in enough malt vinegar to be criminal. Or so Cole liked to say.

She'd be wearing a poncho most of the day if this kept up. Lightning streaked across the sky, and she counted the seconds before the thunderclap followed. It wasn't long, which her mom used to say meant the storm was close.

Water splashed around the guests' feet outside with every step as a gust of wind ruffled their ponchos. Close was a bit of an understatement. It was a good day to go to the theater. Not the most exciting job in the park, helping folks find their seats, but at least the cast was always stellar.

Ellie finished her chips and brushed her fingers off before sitting the basket on the trash can. "Thanks Ana! Are you working at Titania's Table later?"

She shook her head. "I'm covering shifts here for today and tomorrow, at least. Should be back after that."

Ellie waved and pulled the hood of her poncho up, the rain

rattling against it like a thousand tiny feet. Which probably wouldn't have been an unsettling thought if she didn't know so many Fae.

A short, wet walk brought her to the small-scale reproduction of Fairy Glen from Scotland. Forced perspective and incredible detail made it easy to imagine she was standing in another country altogether. The rain didn't hurt the illusion either, as many of the Scottish Fae could be heard lamenting the lack of precipitation in the drier months.

Ellie passed the walkways leading around concentric ridged circles and stones, following the path to the theater. Roman had told her the stones in the real Fairy Glen overseas had been placed there by tourists and existed for years before being removed. But it was something humans often thought were still there, so he added it to the park.

A strong gust of wind blew rain into Ellie's face. She turned away from the breeze and hurried across to the theater, shaking off her poncho before stepping inside.

It was thirty minutes before the next show, but the lobby was already packed with guests. Ellie frowned and slipped through a door to her left, heading backstage to find out why they weren't letting anyone in yet.

She found Hans snoring at a desk, a large wedge of cheese by his nose.

Ellie patted the slibreg on the shoulder. When he didn't respond, she shook him a little and called his name. "Hans!"

Hans bolted upright, blinking rapidly before focusing on Ellie. "What? Is something wrong?"

"The lobby's full of guests because it's raining." Ellie frowned at him. "Is the show ready? Can we let them in?"

Hans rubbed his paws over his eyes. "Not until forty-five minutes before."

"It's less than a half hour before. I think most of the people are just happy to be out of the rain, though."

"I should have gone to sleep earlier last night. They needed help on third shift. I volunteered, but I'm exhausted."

"Just make sure the performers are ready?"

"Already did that." Hans yawned. "I'll double-check the lighting. Be in the sound booth if you need me."

"You're running the sound today, too?" Ellie asked. "Where's Nessa?"

"She'll be here for a later show, I'm sure. Having some software issues at the Mine again."

Ellie hung her poncho on a coat rack along the back wall, grabbed a flashlight, and hurried into the theater proper. In short order, she had the doors unlocked and propped open. She didn't need to tell the guests to come in. As soon as those doors inched apart, they entered like flood water.

Some filed down the incline to the front rows, while others took to the back, staying in the higher seats. There wasn't a bad seat in the house, as far as Ellie could tell in the many times she'd seen the show.

When the theater started filling up, her job became somewhat more involved, asking a few guests to move farther down a row so other families could sit together. It wasn't an issue when attendance was lower, but the rain always filled the theater.

The lights dimmed as the last few guests searched for seats. Ellie led them to rows with her flashlight before heading to the back of the theater. She drummed her fingers on her thigh.

There might be a few more stragglers, but it was time to start the show.

Ellie made her way over to the soundboard, taking a seat beside Hans. He appeared far more alert as he dimmed the runner lights and cued the music. As the crowd quieted, the red velvet curtains peeled back, a single armored Fae standing in the spotlight.

"There was not always peace among the realms, and those destined to maintain it did not always desire to fight in another's war."

The figure on the stage spun, raising their sword to meet another as it struck from the shadows, metal sparking against metal as the crowd cheered and the soldier lunged into shadow.

Lights brightened against the background, showing a painting of brilliant green fields strewn with stones.

"Some soldiers wished to escape the worst of it. Others were never given a chance."

Hans twisted a dial on the effects board and lightning crashed, the stones becoming fallen suits of armor before the thunder receded, and they were only stones once more.

"But as many conflicts do, the war spread beyond our realm. Beyond the farthest reaches of Faerie, to a place the courts had no desire to engage."

A glowing orange ring appeared at the rear of the stage, all other light dimming as an armored shadow stepped through it. The ring vanished, and the light returned in an instant, showing not a field in the background now, but a vast amusement park.

Ellie smiled. Roman had told her the real park from the story had been a simple carnival, but that wasn't grand enough for the theater. Small actors sprinted onto the scene.

"No war stained that place, but there was sadness among its youth. A strange panic at the loss of what our troubled adventurer believed to be a sibling, or perhaps a friend."

The soldier removed his helmet, casting aside his armor and weapons as he kneeled in front of a panicked child.

"What troubles this place, child?"

The brownie portraying the kid wailed, her cry piercing enough that Hans adjusted her microphone. "My bear is gone!"

The narrator returned. "A bear? Our soldier knew what a bear was, and it was certainly no friend to a child."

"A bear, you say?"

"Her stuffed bear," one of the taller humans said as they stepped closer. "She loves it a great deal. His full name is Bear Bear."

"Unfamiliar with what a stuffed bear was," the narrator continued, "our soldier made his decision."

"I will help you find this stuffed bear."

The narrator's voice returned as set pieces rose from beneath the stage and wheeled in from the side, displaying popcorn stands and rides that spun as they crossed in front of the audience. "And so, they hunted, the child's sobs only stopping so she might breathe before resuming their despair. But all was not lost in that strange place, as our soldier found an oddly colored toy on the ground beside a worn tent that could very well represent a bear.

"A small stain dotted its side where it had waited in the mud. A simple swipe of his hand restored it. When he turned to the family again, he held out his discovery.

"'Is this your bear?'

"'Bear Bear!' the child shrieked like a banshee, but it wasn't the sound of loss.

"The family thanked our adventurer and continued on their way, never knowing the impact such a simple joy might have on a soldier bound to war. It was a kind of magic that he did not know in Faerie, and a kind of magic he swore he would help spread in this other realm."

The performer stepped forward. "I was a weapon on the battlefield once, but now I am a shelter for all who ask."

"Some of you may know what came of our brave adventurer," the narrator said.

Backgrounds and the set shifted again, the carnival fading as more familiar things rose behind him: Kraken's Fury, the Bobsled, Titania's Table, and even a distant miniature of the pretzel stand. The last things to arrive were the top hat and the black jacket, which he donned.

"Some of you may know how he built the Theme Park at the End of the World."

The lights cut out. And the applause rose with a fury. A few folks went so far to whistle and cheer before the lights came back on, and the performers took their bows.

Ellie loved the show, but there was something that bothered her about it. Like the story was missing elements or leaving things out. She knew it was Roman's story, but she also knew the Fae were protective of Faerie. She hoped one day Roman might tell her the rest.

THE THEATER WAS nearly empty when the first tornado siren sounded. It was a terrible thing, a grating roar, and one that

Ellie had learned to fear since she was young. As soon as the siren finished, a broadcast echoed over the park's speakers.

"Please find the nearest shelter from the storm. Please calmly and orderly make your way to the basements in Dublin Street, Tinker's Escape, Titania's Table, or the Mine."

The broadcast repeated, but Ellie's radio came to life in a burst of static. Roman's voice, a bitter edge to it. "The sylphs have returned. Those who can help, report to the front gates."

Ellie hurried out the front of the theater, many of the guests making their way to Dublin Street as she veered left, headed toward the gates. There wasn't any question why the tornado sirens had gone off. Sickly green clouds stained the sky until they faded into darkness, and a terrible funnel drifted down in the distance.

It wasn't the only vortex in the area. A lone sylph stood nearby, a spiral of wind and debris, squaring off against Roman outside the gates.

"For your treachery," the sylph hissed.

Roman didn't bother to remove his top hat, though Ellie didn't understand how it was still on his head as the wind bore down on the park.

Cole joined her as she reached the far side of the gates. Manfred and Katinka followed with Bruce, but far more intimidating were Thrud and Yngvarr. The trolls towered over everything else before settling down on either side of Roman, making a rare appearance at a time when humans might spot them.

More of the staff joined Roman, brownies and pookas and many others who had no interest in fighting. They were there in a show of support to Roman, but the thickening funnel cloud would be on them in minutes, its debris field increasing with every passing moment.

Roman projected his voice, and it echoed through the air, uncanny, unsettling. "Sylphs. I am bound no longer by the rules of that foolish war. No matter what you bring against me, I will protect this place and all who dwell within."

"Your treachery will not go unpunished. You betrayed the clans, betrayed your kingdom, and all who visit this place will fall for your crimes."

"Leave." Roman gave them time to turn away. To redirect the storm that would bring ruin and death onto the park and so many of its guests.

Still, it barreled toward them. Ellie and Cole huddled behind the trolls when the first heavy debris crashed into Thrud's hand.

"Have you forgotten my name?" Roman's voice rose to a thunder, all vestiges of humanity peeled away as he strode forward in a moment of rage. He held his hand out, fingers down like a claw as the gale ripped at his coat. The air pulsed as if alive with a beating heart until Roman threw his hand into the air, and the earth cracked. Stone and dirt and rock shot into the sky like a cannon, piercing the debris cloud and the very heart of the tornado.

Ellie heard the screams, saw the Fae fall from the air. A dozen or more clutched at wounds that blackened and raced through their bodies as the tornado bent and then broke as it dissipated. She looked back to Roman, the anger replaced with something else. Replaced with sadness, as though he had once more become what he never wanted to be.

His voice was only a whisper. "I was the Iron Blade."

Chills ran down Ellie's spine. It wasn't dirt and stone Roman had called from the earth. It was iron. For the Fae, it was death. And the words from the play in the theater came back into her mind.

"I was a weapon on the battlefield once, but now I am a shelter for all who ask."

Ellie pulled away from Cole and rushed forward, throwing her arms around Roman and squeezing him tight. At first, he didn't respond. Didn't look away from the destruction he'd unleashed on those who would have attacked his people, his family. Slowly, his arms embraced her, and Roman, the Iron Blade, rested his chin on her head.

She heard Gus whispering behind them. "That's why you don't steal his churros."

Chapter 20

"A TERRIBLE HAILSTORM in the county today. Violent enough to leave divots across a field for nearly half a mile. Theme park lovers will be glad to know the Theme Park at the End of the World avoided the worst of the storm, only losing a few signs to the wind and outskirts of the hail. We'll have more on this evening's news."

Ana turned the volume down and placed the remote on the bar. "Well, that's a relief. Last thing we need is a bunch of conspiracy folks showing up at the park again."

"Again?" Ellie asked around a mouthful of mac n cheese bites.

"Ask Roman." Ana nodded to Ellie like he was standing in the room.

"Ellie?"

She shrieked and spun toward the voice just behind her. "Roman, why do you do that?"

"I felt it was less invasive than tapping you on the shoulder."

Ellie didn't really have a good argument at that point, so she let it drop. "Any problems with the guests from yesterday?"

Roman shook his head. "We secured them all in the storm shelters in time. No one saw what happened. No one sustained injury. I am grateful to all of you who helped."

"Can I ask you something?" Ellie glanced away before returning her focus to Roman. "About the show in the theater?"

"Of course." Roman gestured to Ana. "Could you bring two of the latest cut comb milkshakes to our table, Ana?"

"Will do."

"They don't serve those here, Roman." Ellie frowned at him. "Are you going to make her walk all the way to Titania's Table?"

"Come, Ellie. Sit with me and speak. And no, Ana always has milkshakes ready at every restaurant. A secret I have shared with few."

"*Please* don't tell everyone." Ana laughed as she came around the bar, carrying a pair of milkshakes and setting the glasses on a table in the corner.

Ellie followed her over, sliding in one side while Roman took the other.

"What is it you'd like to ask?"

"Is it all true? I mean, how you came here and started the park? The war between the Fae?"

"It all happened, yes, but I do not know if I would call it *true*."

Ellie sipped at her milkshake. "What do you mean?"

A long sigh escaped Roman's lips before he turned his milkshake between his fingers. "War stays with you. The battle, the stress. It is never entirely gone. We have that wretched trait in common with humans. But the show … yes. I have told you before a mission brought me to your realm, into a carnival."

Ellie nodded.

"The story in our theater is a much kinder thing, Ellie." He paused, his brow furrowing briefly. "There was a battle in that place. A great fire that cost many lives, both human and Fae."

She sat up straighter as Roman continued. Ellie remembered the news from years before, the stories of those who had been lost, but she never imagined it could have been a part of Faerie's conflicts.

"There *was* a child there, and true to my word, I have told a great many souls about the triumphs of her Bear Bear. I cannot express to you how, in that moment, in such a time of horror, that child was still so happy just to get a small stuffed creature returned to her. It is a memory that returned every day thereafter."

Roman took a long drink of his milkshake and glanced away. "It was not all good, Ellie. We tried to save more humans, but they were lost to the battles, caught in the flames conjured by our enemies. We spared some from the inferno, but we could not save them all."

"You tried." Ellie reached for his hand before holding back. "That means a lot."

"Perhaps. It meant enough to my allies. We were no benevolent force in that place, Ellie. We still had a mission, though it changed when we saw what had been done. There had been so much happiness in that carnival before the battle grew. It spoke to us of a distance from the War of Realms. A different life, if we could only end that foolish conflict.

"I had a friend at the battle, who you may have heard spoken of in the park before. I do not know. Ben sacrificed himself to throw down their leader. He sacrificed himself to destroy an empire, to save a young human."

Roman turned his glass between his fingers, meeting Ellie's gaze. "There is no glory, child. There is only memory."

She sat in silence for a time, waiting for him to continue. Ellie didn't want to say the wrong thing, didn't want Roman to stop talking. She'd never heard these stories, and she wanted to know more.

"Walk with me, Ellie. I want you to see the legacy he left."

Chapter 21

ROMAN LEFT A series of gold coins on the table for Ana, then led the way out of the pub. They continued down Dublin Street and through Fairy Glen, crossing into Merrows Lagoon and finally taking the path through the Dark Forest.

Ellie glanced back when they passed the HR building and corporate towers when she heard voices. It was just Gus and Capy walking between buildings. Roman stepped to the rear gates, sliding them open and gesturing for her to follow. A narrow trail vanished into the fallen leaves and wood, growing steep as he led them deeper into the forest, every step crunching as they went.

"There is something you don't know about these hills, Ellie. An old soul who will watch over this place for all time."

"What do you mean?"

Roman smiled at her. "Ben was a giant, and not like the trolls, but one from the ancient tales. He was always fond of this realm in life."

Ellie frowned. "Ben was here before the war?"

He nodded. "Many times, Ellie. And now, like many of the giants, Ben will be a part of this land until the end of the world." Roman slowed as he crested the next hill and waited for Ellie.

Before his comments, she would have thought nothing of

the ravine before them. But now, she searched for clues and details and gasped when she found them.

"The cave? Is that … a skull?"

Roman nodded. "I know it may be grim in your eyes, Ellie, but I know he would be happy here."

Her gaze traveled the length of the hill from the caves to the twisted plateau that had clearly been a giant's legs in the past, but they looked no different from the limestone bluffs and caverns she'd known when she was younger.

"He took me sledding when we were young Fae. The only person I ever called friend. Until I met the humans he protected. Until I met you and those who would come to this park. He died saving Cole in what would be the final battle we were a part of in the War of Realms."

"What? Here?"

"Yes. The story from the play, Ellie. That carnival was held here in the fields not far from the road." Roman crouched, gesturing to the hillside. "We called him Ben at his request. He liked to say he was related to the giant who tore up the causeway between Ireland and Scotland long ago." A smile crossed the old Fae's face. "He also indulged in many a tall tale in the years I knew him."

"He saved Cole?"

Roman stood. "The family Cole was meant to infiltrate, but never had the chance, Ellie. They died in the battle alongside many others in that tragedy. It is rare for a changeling to survive that kind of loss. Even when they do, they are stunned, like a terrified animal. Ben pulled Cole and several humans off the field of battle, sheltering them in these hills. In this place. It cost him everything."

Pressure built behind Ellie's eyes. She didn't know Ben, couldn't imagine what motivated the giant, but without him she never would have met Cole. Without him and Roman, she wouldn't have her home, her *family*, at the park.

Roman squeezed her shoulder. "Do not weep for the lost Ellie. Celebrate them, speak of them often, so their memory may persevere through the ages. It is something I need to do more, and perhaps a change I will have made to our play."

"Why didn't you do that already?"

He gave her a small smile. "Because loss is hard, Ellie. Even for the Fae."

COLE FROZE WITH an empanada stuffed halfway into his mouth at the bar in Titania's Table. "He told you about Ben?"

Ellie nodded and sipped at her dragon pearl tea sweetened with clover honey.

"Wow. I didn't think he'd ever tell anyone who wasn't there about that. I mean, you've seen the play how many times now?"

"He talked about changing the play to include his story."

Cole took another bite of empanada and shook his head. "Help me eat these, will you?"

"Twist my arm." Ellie flashed Cole a grin and picked up an empanada. Still warm and crisp when she bit into it, and there was something to be said for the beef steak filling with onions, potatoes, and carrots. Such a small package for a remarkably rich filling.

She shook the empanada at Cole and sat up. "This has potatoes in it!"

He slowly raised an eyebrow.

"I don't think the Taters have ever reviewed it. I need to text them."

"Ellie, you're going to keep them in food ideas forever."

"Good, then I won't have to rewatch as many episodes."

Cole smiled and sipped at his milkshake. "He told you about my family, too?"

Ellie wasn't sure how to respond. She knew enough about changelings to know what they were supposed to do. Were they bound as tightly as a regular family at that point? She wasn't sure, and she didn't want to ask Cole now. So soon after he'd had to reveal his secret to her.

Instead, she nodded.

"I never got to know them. I don't know what would have happened if I had. Did Roman tell you about it? The fire, I mean?"

"A little. At the carnival?"

"Yeah. You know their kid is still alive? Did he tell you that?"

Ellie leaned back. "What? How?"

"Ben saved him." Cole lowered his voice. "Not all change-lings just stole people, Ellie. Some of us were there to do other things."

"Like what?"

"Like bring a human to Faerie to heal. There are so many things humans can get sick from, and there are so many ways the Fae can heal them. Sometimes it takes years, though, and that's a hard thing to explain, isn't it?"

"What do you do to get them back?"

Cole swirled his straw. "Sometimes they never go back. By choice. Other times, their memories are taken by Fae who feed on that sort of thing."

Liam cleared his throat behind the bar. "Cole."

The changeling flashed him a smile. "It's fine, Liam. Roman told her about Ben."

Liam blinked. "Truly? Well, carry on then. Try not to scare her off, though." The bartender winked at Ellie.

Ellie chewed on the last of her empanada and chased it with tea. Another idea struck her. "So, you sometimes bring them back with amnesia?"

"Yes! Exactly. I mean, sometimes amnesia is just a human problem, but other times …" Cole shrugged.

"Like when Roman gave me too much magic in a churro and I stared at a puddle for an hour?"

Liam barked out a laugh as he wiped down the bar. "I hadn't heard about that! Oh, that's good."

"I don't know if I'd say it was *good*," Ellie muttered.

Cole grinned at her. "Kind of like that."

"I swear I need a vacation after this week. There's been so much happening in the park, Cole."

"If you took a vacation, where would you go?"

"Here," Ellie said sheepishly.

Cole reached out and squeezed her arm. "It's like a whole new park now that you can ride at night, isn't it?"

"In a lot of ways, it is. In a lot of ways, it still just feels right. Although I wouldn't mind traveling to some other parks. Maybe we can convince Roman to pay for us to travel." She clasped her hands together. "In the name of research?"

Glasses clinked together as Liam refilled the racks. "You're a devious one, Ellie. I appreciate that."

"I think we should try it." Cole rapped his knuckles on the

bar top. "Worst thing he says is no, right?"

"Okay, but not yet. Detailed planning starts for Halloween next week, and I have some great ideas for the Dark Park houses this year."

"Oh, really?"

A wicked grin etched itself across Ellie's lips. "If Roman will let us do it, I don't think the Fae will ever forget it."

Cole rubbed his hands together. "I love it already."

Chapter 22

ELLIE KNEW ROMAN didn't want every house to be *too* scary at Dark Park, being that he still wanted Fae and humans both to venture inside, but he did give his blessing to Capy and the slibreg to work with the creative team on her idea for Titania's Curse. Roman also wanted humans to believe everything inside could be built by mortal hands. So, instead of using magic to mimic it, he'd actually hired contractors to build the basics of the house.

It only took them two weeks to construct the supporting structure of each one, but it would be another two before the Fae finished decorating every scene. Ellie looked up at the façade, beautiful clusters of wooden flowers set across the front with the flowing letters of Titania's Blessing spelled out in glowing lights. A bloody red streak cut through the word *Blessing* and *Curse* had been scrawled over it.

The sign for the entrance would be much the same when it was revealed along the path by Dublin Street. She couldn't wait to see it lit with the wait times as fog machines filled the area.

"Ellie."

She glanced to the side to find Roman, sharply dressed in black slacks and a loose jacket with a bit too much intricate embroidery to be casual.

"Show me what you and the team have done."

Ellie's smile grew. He was clearly ready for their walkthrough. "You're going to hate it."

"That is my concern."

She led the way through the arch of wooden flowers. The lights were still on, but music played in the background, a quiet pulse of bass and drums with the whine of a cello's highest registers searing through the treble.

Some of the houses that year had vocal tracks that played on loops, but Titania's Curse went a different direction. Here, the story unfolded with the set pieces, enhanced by the soundtrack as some of her legends were laid out in earnest, only they had been twisted into their darkest versions.

A single word glowed against a wall of scenery. Blessings. Trees and vibrant pastures, almost impossibly green in their coloration, detailed beyond reason, framed a simple animatronic of the queen. A brilliant white gown spread out behind her, woven with flowering vines and blooms.

Roman's gaze snapped to the side when they hit the first trigger, the floor vibrating beneath their feet when wood cracked against wood. There was no other scare in that room, and they moved into the hall. Even in the light, Ellie could see the spring colors shift and pale, growing to fall, and then to something unnaturally dark.

"This is Betrayal. It might be my favorite room!"

Roman eyed the murals on the wall, lit to give the illusion of stained glass. Each showed the progression of a cloaked form attempting to assassinate Titania. "There are many who have tried through the ages, Ellie."

"I didn't need to know that." She gestured ahead of them. "See the ledge up there?"

He nodded.

"We have a bungee rig, so one of our scare actors can drop down over people like they're falling. But it rights them as soon as they reach the edge." She pointed to a stone well beside the designated path. "And if that doesn't catch them, there's a blood siren in the well."

"A … what?"

"Shay's idea, apparently. That's what Franzi told me. It's an old legend that comes from poisoned wells, I think?"

"I'm not familiar with it. Perhaps it is regional to those who have moved here." He studied the detail on the well. "Will the mermaids be taking shifts here?"

Ellie nodded. "Kraken's Fury is shutting down for the cold anyway, so a few of the cast have already volunteered."

The hallway darkened along with the music, the distant sound of hammers and nail guns working nearby breaking the mood. The third room was bleak. Not only from the lack of light, but every flower and tree and bush inside that place was blackened with rot. The few animals in the room were only carcasses, remnants of fur and flesh and bone.

"We'll add some ghosts and special effects in, and this room will be *packed* with scare actors. The last room isn't built out yet, but it should be by tomorrow."

"Ellie." Roman's eyebrow rose as he looked up at the fury of a mad queen.

Red eyes glared down at all who entered that place, hands raised as flames danced across them. There was still beauty in that visage, but it sent shivers down Ellie's spine, and she knew it would send Fae screaming.

"It's great, right?"

He let out a long breath. "We're going to need to add a warning to the entryway for the Fae."

"That'll only make it more popular!"

"If you say it is so, Ellie."

She grinned at him, not correcting his slightly mangled use of the human saying. "I did have another idea."

"Oh?"

"Some of the other parks do a media night, you know?"

Roman didn't quite hide his grimace. "I have no wish to bring news stations and lighting rigs and more chaos into the park, Ellie."

"No, no, I mean small-scale. Like for the vloggers! Let them try the seasonal food and cover it on social media for you." She gestured with excitement. "It'll generate more interest. Remember how much busier Titania's Table got after the Taters released their video?"

Roman slowly rubbed his chin. "I will think on it, Ellie. Events such as that are not without their costs, and not everything in this park is paid in gold." He eyed the surrounding room. "You know, some of the Fae can see well enough in the dark they will notice some of this rigging. If there is time, the crew could hide more of it. Make the illusion of the forest more complete."

"Great idea! I'll have them get right on that."

Roman hesitated, and for once, Ellie felt like *she* had finally tricked *him* into doing exactly what she wanted for the house.

"Cole!" As soon as Roman left, Ellie hurried into the last room where the largest construction was still taking place. "Roman said yes!"

Cole glanced over his shoulder. "That's fantastic, Ellie. Give me just a second." He levered a long piece of rough timber into place and Thrud secured it with two flicks of her thumbnail.

Thrud's voice filled the room. "It is almost time for our break, Cole. Let us retire for the evening."

"Sounds like a great idea. Especially before we pin you into the corner again."

Thrud laughed as she crouched down and exited through the rear of the tent. Well, they called it a tent, but it had a longer name: tension fabric structure. But no one wanted to remember that. Far more durable than anything you'd take camping, that was for sure.

Cole dusted his hands off. He still had jeans and a flannel shirt on, just like anything else he would have worn before Ellie knew he was a changeling. "What?"

She beamed at him. "Nothing. Just happy we got away with it. Titania's Curse!"

"I'm excited to see how the last room turns out. It's a heck of a twist, Ellie. Sometimes I wonder how your brain works."

"Oddly, apparently." She shouldered him to the side.

LESS THAN A week passed before Roman called Ellie into his office in HR. It was rare for him to take any kind of meeting there, so she worried it was going to be bad news.

"Take a seat, please."

Roman's office wasn't much nicer than the individual cubicles the rest of the staff occupied. That wasn't a bad thing, though, as the cubicles were quite nice in their own way. One sizable difference was the desk, a heavy thing full of knots and whorls, stained as dark as the night.

Ellie settled into the wheeled office chair opposite him, its breathable mesh backing contrasting with the darker tones of the room.

"I wanted to tell you in person, Ellie. I have approved your idea for a media night."

Ellie blinked. "Really? I mean, that's wonderful, Roman! Where should we do the tasting? How many people should we invite? I mean, there are so many vloggers and writers we could invite. But we don't want to overwhelm the other guests."

Roman held up his hands in surrender. "I'll leave many of these choices to you and Cole, Ellie. With feedback from Hans and Franzi, particularly. We need to be sure we are able to meet the demand of an entire season."

"Titania's Table." Ellie nodded as she spoke. "We can do the tasting in the garden! Line up a buffet, or some catering tables like we have in the café? You know we might need a tent if it's outdoors, though. If it rains, that would ruin everything." She paused and tapped her chin. "Or it could add to the mood!"

Roman offered a small smile. "I am quite certain rain would indeed ruin the food."

"We need a new Potato on a Stick. Something weird. Maybe one that tastes like candy corn?"

To Roman's credit, he didn't wince at the idea. "Perhaps you should meet with Hans and Franzi. Terrible minds think alike, as they say."

Ellie hesitated. "I'll do that. Thanks, Roman. This is going to be great!"

HANS SCRIBBLED DOWN the third idea for a new potato on a stick while Ellie and Franzi watched. The whiteboard at the back of the test kitchen had been erased so many times without a good cleaning it had the faded remnants of dozens of recipes.

Franzi read the current ideas out loud. "Candy corn. Cotton candy. Sour candy."

"Every idea is candy," Hans said. "We need savory options, too."

"Why don't we try some of these first?" Ellie asked. "I think they'd be fun."

Hans put his paws on his hips and stared at the board. "Fine, fine. Franzi. Make the sour candy flavor. I'll work on the candy corn and cotton candy."

"Leave me the hard one." Franzi sniffed and wiggled her nose at Hans. "I see how you work."

"You're the master of complex concoctions, my dear. I, on the other hand, know how to make things sweet."

"Including your excuses." Franzi grinned at him. "Ellie, could you grab another bag of potatoes out of the cellar? I'll prepare the potion."

"Sure!" Ellie hopped up out of her chair and walked to the stairwell at the back of the kitchen. The staircase followed a shallow curve before opening onto a wide rack of wines and several baskets set into dark wooden shelves.

She found a burlap sack of potatoes past the turnips and parsnips, waiting beneath drying sprigs of various spices. Ellie grabbed several potatoes and headed back up the stairs, her boots thudding on every step before she made it back to the kitchen.

"Perfect." Franzi gestured for the potatoes. "Could you give them a quick wash?"

Ellie dropped the armful of tubers into the sink and turned the water on. She grabbed a vegetable brush and got to work while she watched Franzi carefully measure out a series of clear liquids, each adding a different color to a syringe when the slibreg combined them.

Franzi sniffed at the tincture and frowned. "A little too harsh still, I believe. I doubt Roman would want to cause actual pain from the sour notes."

"I can try it!" Ellie said, switching out potatoes in the sink.

"Not yet. You might not be able to taste anything else for a week."

"Candy corn!" Hans said, scooping up the first of Ellie's potatoes. He injected the long needle of a syringe into the vegetable and moved it to the cutting board. His whiskers twitched before he said, "You didn't see this."

Flames flickered in the slibreg's paw, licking up around the potato as he turned it in his claws.

"You can—"

"No," Franzi said. "As Hans already said, you didn't see anything." She cocked a furry eyebrow at the other slibreg as he dragged a knife through the potato, offering each of them a taste.

Ellie juggled the sample in her hand for a second while it cooled down, then took a bite. Hans and Franzi did the same, chewing for all of two seconds before freezing, turning to the trash can, and spitting everything out.

Ellie managed to finish her bite, working through the sickly-sweet flavor of brown sugar mashed up with creamed corn, but not without making what she imagined to be a very unflattering expression. She swallowed and offered a weak smile. "That is not candy corn."

Hans walked over to the whiteboard and erased it.

"Now, if we could just erase that from our tongues," Franzi muttered.

Hans and Ellie both grinned at her.

Chapter 23

ELLIE BOUNCED ON her heels, waiting close to the entrance signage to Titania's Curse. It was the first house on the media tour, and she couldn't wait to see Tottie and Poe again. Months had passed since they crossed paths with anything more than a cursory wave or greeting.

The music loop reset, bass thumping through the land before a stuttering pizzicato crept through the air. Some of the other lands had tracks with brutal distortion and heavy guitars, but the land around Titania's Curse was subtler, creepier, and remarkably unsettling. By the time the drums kicked in, a whine of wooden bows on worn strings joined the cacophony.

She saw more than one vlogger cringing before they'd even set foot inside the house. Part of that might have been the pooka, decked out in bloody Halloween costumes and stalking their guests through the shadows, those wide black eyes far more ominous in the dark.

"Ellie!"

She turned toward the voice, finding Tottie in a shirt from last year's Dark Park event. Poe followed behind her, tracking a pooka dressed in all black except for a rotting orange pumpkin mask. The pooka lunged, and Tottie screeched, her space buns bouncing as she sprinted at Ellie.

"They are *so good* this year, Ellie."

Poe laughed as he lowered the camera and stepped up beside her. "Pretty sure I caught all that. Priceless."

"How are you two?" Ellie asked, beaming. "I'm so glad you could make it tonight; I can't even tell you. Anyway, we have time to go through a house before they start serving food. You want to try it?"

"Lead on, Ellie." Tottie gave a flourish of her hand. "But first, hugs." She embraced her before stepping to the side so Ellie could hug Poe.

"Where's Cole?" Poe asked.

"He wanted to work as a scare actor tonight. You'll probably see him." She grinned, knowing what was waiting in Titania's Curse. "Let's go!"

"Wait, which house? Where are we going to see him?"

Ellie didn't answer with anything more than a sly smile.

They followed the winding queue to the tent set up backstage. It was one of the few times guests got a peek behind the scenes of the park, and she didn't miss Poe taking some footage of the shadowy paths.

Ellie couldn't have been happier with the façade at night, the wooden flowers creating an unsettling texture beneath the neon glow of the sign. The archway had been finished, flickering lights leading them down the path to the entrance.

Tottie went first, followed closely by Ellie. Poe trailed behind with the camera, ready to catch every jump and scream. Even though Ellie had helped design parts of the house, she didn't think she'd be able to stop herself from screaming if the scare actors were really on their game. And she doubted Poe would edit the footage in any kind of flattering way. A screech got more views than a casual stroll. The price of being friends with vloggers.

They followed the line of guests through the arch of wooden flowers. Music was no subtle feature now, almost deafening in volume as the bass vibrated through her. They'd worked on the mix, and Ellie didn't miss the haunting echoes Nessa had added to the tracks.

Ellie yelped when a white gown appeared from nothing, thrusting flowers toward Tottie as a scare actor came within inches of her. Lights flashed, and the form changed to a smiling Fae with a simple offering. The blessings sign along the wall brightened, warming the room, but making the colors of the trees and pastures wrong. Every vlogger ahead of them slowed and took extra footage of the welcoming animatronic queen. Her flowering vines and blooms formed a stunning visage in the darkness.

Poe shouted behind them when wood crashed against wood, shaking the floor beneath their feet. The hall beyond faded from the eerie red light to near-total darkness. A boom sounded beside her, and claws reached through the shadows. Ellie shrieked and jumped away, uncanny laughter echoing around them. She'd forgotten they'd added a boo hole there.

The hallway opened onto Betrayal. Ellie clapped her hands as everyone in that line paused, taking in the murals, the detailed artwork featuring cloaked forms of assassins and Titania striking them down.

Heavy breathing echoed through the audio, and lightning cracked above them, showing the cloak of an assassin as they fell forward, blade outstretched. Tottie screamed like a banshee before the bungees caught Cole and pulled him back up onto his ledge. And just like that, the scare reset, the darkness so absolute no one would see a scare actor looming above them.

"That was Cole!" Ellie shouted to Tottie with a laugh.

"You're kidding!" She flashed a wide smile at Ellie. "That was amazing. I'm going to kill him."

Ellie's gaze immediately dropped to the stone well. She hadn't seen what was coming. Only saw them working on the costume in Merrows Lagoon.

An air cannon blasted the guests as they neared the well, clawed, webbed fingers leaping from the shallow well as a grotesque form lunged at them all, sweeping her arms wide. The siren's scales looked as if they'd been torn and ripped, gory slashes running across her delicate face as she slammed her hands down on the stone and leaned forward, a piercing scream on her lips.

Every single person in that room shrieked except Ellie. Ellie laughed and clapped and almost jumped up and down. The siren pointed at them as she slowly sank back into the well.

Poe cursed behind them, and Ellie wasn't sure if she'd ever felt more proud.

The next hall took a hard right, thin trails of thread and fabric hanging from the ceiling so it felt as though something was touching you in the dark. Even knowing what it was, the sensation unsettled Ellie.

In front of her, Tottie shouted, jumping back as a boo hole dropped open, and a ghostly form waited inside, reaching toward them. As soon as she turned away, the other side of the hall opened onto a massive boo hole, and a thunderous crack echoed around them as the door fell. A group of four mangled spirits drifted in the light.

"Oh, I hope that shows up on the video," Poe said behind

them.

The last room was a nightmare. Every flower, every *piece* of flora, dripped with blood and black ooze. Bones rose from the beds, long dead things that had rotted away in the turning of the seasons. Scrawled across the wall was a simple word: *fury*.

They had all of two seconds to take it in before the scare actors struck. One after another, dressed as skeletons, cloaked assassins, rotting zombies. They moved with purpose and speed, closing on different ranks and guests until the entire room was screaming and laughing, and only when they'd reached a crescendo did the lights in the floor explode into life to reveal the last room.

More beautiful than Ellie had imagined. A true fairy queen in all her glory. Whoever they'd hired to perform as Titania was perfect. With the makeup and sweeping gown, her flowering crown set with gleaming sapphires, it was jarring at the least. She didn't have the ominous red glow of the animatronic's eyes, but everything else was more than Ellie could have hoped for.

Guest after guest left that room clapping, talking about how they couldn't wait to visit the house again. How it might be their new favorite.

Tottie turned back to Ellie and Poe. "I don't even know what to say."

Ellie grinned at her, and then the camera.

"I need time to process," Poe said, spinning the camera around so he could film the trio at once. "You all need to see this. It's ... just get down to the Theme Park at the End of the World. If you're a Halloween fan, it's not to be missed!"

Poe lowered the camera and shook his head. "That last

scene? Ellie!"

"I know!" Ellie squeezed her hands together, her words almost a squeak. "I hadn't seen it finished. Blew my expectations away. I have to find out who they hired for Titania."

"I thought it was an animatronic?" Tottie asked.

"If it was, it was the best I've ever seen," Poe said.

Ellie spotted Cole in his assassin's garb, standing by the exit. It must have been time for a shift change. "I'll be right back, you two." She hurried over to him. "Cole, who's playing Titania in there? She's amazing!"

Cole frowned at her. "We didn't hire anyone to play Titania."

"Shut up, yes you did."

He gave her a lost look.

"Poe. Poe!" Ellie gestured for the Taters to come back. "Can we see that last scene on the camera?"

"Sure thing." Poe started looking for the clip as he walked over.

"Cole was telling me we missed something about Titania."

"I'm sure the camera picked it up." Poe swiped forward to the reveal of the last room. And there, centered on the screen, was a stiff animatronic. Attractive, polished, and refined, but it wasn't what she'd seen in the room.

"Weird," Tottie said. "I swear that looked a lot better in the moment. Didn't her crown shine? Must be the ISO on the camera. Blew it out."

Ellie froze. "I'll … I'll be right back. Wait for me!"

She ran to the exit, groups of laughing creators and vloggers coming out with their cameras and phones. Ellie slipped inside in a gap, nodding to the exit attendant. Sure enough, the final room looked different. There was no glorious crown or flowing hair in an unfelt breeze. That hadn't been an illusion or a trick of the light at all.

Ellie shuffled backward and almost sprinted out of the house, shrieking when someone grabbed her. She looked up just in time to stop herself from panicking. Roman stood there with a wide smile on his face.

"Ellie."

"Roman! Something's weird. We saw a different last room. The animatronic looked … more real? I can't explain it. I just—"

"Slow down, Ellie. You caught the eye of Titania."

She couldn't speak. He said it so calmly, as if it wasn't a nightmare come to life.

"It is not so bad a thing." He patted her shoulder twice. "She found great amusement with the house you assembled, though had some minor quibbles with the story on the murals."

"What?" Ellie's heart hammered in her chest.

Roman smiled and ushered her along. "Go, enjoy the tasting with your friends tonight. You've done well, Ellie. And this night will be celebrated for many years to come."

She didn't look back at Roman. Barely acknowledged Cole when he put his arm around her shoulders.

"Did he just say that was Titania?" Cole whispered.

Ellie nodded. "And that we should just go eat with the Taters."

Cole whistled as he walked her back to Tottie and Poe. "I guess we did alright on the house."

Ellie blinked.

"I need a break." Cole's voice was even, and sounded far calmer than Ellie felt. "Let's go get some food. If Roman said you should go get food, in my experience, you're fine. If he tells you to run and hide in an iron box for a week, that's when you should worry."

Ellie let a small laugh slip at that absurd idea. She took a deep breath and nodded. "Okay, let's go eat."

ELLIE HADN'T SEEN what had been done to the garden outside Titania's Table, but she wasn't disappointed as the group walked out the back doors of the restaurant and into another world. The food waited off to the right, meticulously organized with little placards declaring what each dish was.

The center of the garden remained untouched, both by décor and lighting, which made for a surreal darkness, lit only by the spotlight on the statue of Titania. To their left were a dozen round tables, each large enough to seat ten at once. With the standing tables closer to the building, they had more space than Ellie thought they'd need.

Each centerpiece was themed to one of the houses or scare zones, and Ellie wanted to hug Capy. She'd done an amazing job organizing the entire thing. The food might have been almost all on Hans and Franzi, but Capy had run with the decorations.

"Blinky cups!" Poe hurried toward the bar.

Tottie sighed. "I think we lost him." She tilted her head to the side. "What's that creepy music, Ellie?"

She smiled and listened to the skipping melody of eighth notes and sixteenth notes before they slowed between phrases. "'King of the Fairies.' It's an old Celtic song. Although, I think they might have messed with the key on this one."

Tottie shivered. "Let's get some food. Poe can catch up."

Ellie didn't even need to read the sign before she snatched a pepperoni pizza skull pretzel. She scooped up a basket of churros cut at random angles and covered in chocolate and syrupy strawberries. Ellie glanced down the row of food and realized she might not be able to try everything if she grabbed too much on her first run.

Balancing the pretzel skull and churros, she snatched up one last snack, a triangular sambusa stuffed with lamb and onion and beets. It didn't look much like Halloween until you bit into it, and found the beets had dyed everything a menacing shade of red.

"You know what they need to do next year?" Poe asked as he joined them in line.

Ellie glanced back. "What's that?"

"Give them weird names. A lot of the parks do that. Whatever season it is. You know, gory sambusas or burnt skull pretzels."

"You'll have to excuse him," Tottie said. "He's not the most creative when it comes to naming things."

Poe huffed.

"It's a good idea, though," Cole said from the end of the buffet line. He gestured with a deep-fried peanut butter sandwich drizzled with hot honey.

Franzi walked out from behind one of the tall, heated holding cabinets as she pulled her gloves off. "I love that idea. I'll ask Roman about it."

"For the holidays?" Ellie asked.

She nodded and her whiskers twitched. "I think it's a perfect time to try it." She pawed at the tip of her nose before washing her hands in a portable sink. "We're only in the first day of Halloween, though, so perhaps we could do some this season, too." Franzi glanced at Poe. "But not gory sambusas, thank you."

Tottie laughed as Franzi pulled her gloves on again and went back to work at the outdoor fryers.

"How do they do that?" Poe asked. "I mean, even the whiskers twitch on that costume. It's amazing. And if I didn't know better, I'd think they were actually cooking right here in front of us."

Hans raised an eyebrow from the far station and Ellie gave him an awkward grin.

"Weird, right? Let's eat."

They settled in at a far table. The light wasn't *too* red there, so Poe thought he'd be able to get some decent footage.

Ellie picked up the pizza pretzel skull from the red-streaked beer cheese. Poe tried to get the perfect shot of the cheese dripping back into the bowl on his own skull, but Tottie finally snatched it away and bit half the head off.

"Hey!"

"Hey what?" Tottie slowed and closed her eyes. "Oh my, oh my. Try this, Poe!" She thrust the half-eaten skull back at him.

Ellie took a bite of hers. A crisp exterior filled with pepperoni and mozzarella mingled with the yeasty notes of the beer cheese. "So good."

"Right?" Tottie said.

Poe was speechless, savoring the last bite as he finished the snack.

Cole slid his peanut butter sandwich to Ellie before stealing the basket of churros. "I'm surprised you're finally eating more churros."

"Why weren't you eating churros?" Tottie asked.

Ellie glared at Poe. "Long story. I just burned out on them a bit. I had one I thought was cinnamon, but it was actually, uh, chocolate? Just threw me off."

"No judgment here," Poe said. "We have a niece who only eats chicken nuggets. And not the high-quality ones. Those are 'fancy chickens' and clearly not for eating. In fact, if it's been smashed into a mold of some creature it definitely isn't, even better. Especially dinosaurs."

Tottie snorted a laugh. "That's true."

Ellie bit into the peanut butter sandwich, the breading crunching in her mouth before the sweet notes of honey and peanut butter mingled on her tongue. She stared at the odd concoction. "What's spicy on this? Why is this so good?"

"Hot honey." Cole stuffed some of the diced churros into his mouth. "These are great, too!"

Tottie slowly tore a sambusa in two, steam curling up as Poe filmed it. She handed half to Ellie and split the rest with Poe. It certainly didn't look appetizing with the beets blended into the filling, having more the appearance of a horror movie prop than food, but it smelled amazing.

Ellie wasn't sure how it would taste after eating something as rich and sticky as a fried peanut butter sandwich, but the sambusa was perfection. The wrapper crunched between her teeth, the lamb and onion filling rich enough to feel decadent before an earthy note of the beets hit as an aftertaste, mingling with subtle notes of coriander.

Cole, being the more pragmatic of the group, had already gone back for seconds. "Anybody else want another one?"

Ellie shook her head. "No, bring me the pizza tots!"

"There are pizza tots?" Poe rubbed his hands together, turning to Tottie. "I need you to—"

"No."

"But you—"

"No."

"It's going to happen, Tottie. You need to eat pizza tots on camera."

She balled up a napkin and sighed. "Do you remember how many memes popped up last time I ate tots on camera?"

"It was amazing," Ellie whispered.

Tottie placed a hand over her heart. "I am betrayed. Why hast thou forsaken me?"

Poe snorted and threw Cole a thumbs up for tots.

Cole came back a short time later, two small baskets of pizza tots in one hand and two miniature milkshakes in the other, the interior of the glasses streaked with red goo.

"Pizza tots and strawberry honey milkshakes." Cole passed them around the table.

Poe waggled an eyebrow at Tottie. "Come on. Just one for the camera."

"You could do a whole intro on it!" Ellie said. "*Taters' Rides and Guides* with Tottie tasting Tater Tots."

"Brilliant." Poe nodded in appreciation.

Tottie narrowed her eyes. "You're all getting fed to the scare actors later." She jabbed her fork into the pizza tots and took an angry bite. Her scowl didn't last long.

Ellie knew why as soon as she took a bite of her own. It tasted so much like the sauce from the pizza pretzels she did a double take. But instead of a salty pretzel, it came with buttery fried nuggets of potatoes.

"Give us your Tater Tot take, Tottie," Poe said.

Tottie skewered another tot with a chunk of pepperoni on top. "Look, you all know I don't like eating tots on camera. But I'm telling you right now, get down to the Theme Park at the End of the World and put this in your face." She took a huge bite, clearing her entire fork before laughing and covering her mouth.

Poe didn't turn the camera away until Tottie finally waved him off. Only then did he break down in a cackling laugh. "That was so good!"

Ellie leaned in conspiratorially. "So, you want to finish those milkshakes and check out another house?"

"Yes!" the Taters chorused.

ELLIE WAS TORN on doing the Carnival Carnage house or Undead Empire, but in the end, she opted for the latter. They'd make it to all the houses eventually, and Undead Empire was a little less gross right after dinner.

The entrance loomed over them as they reached Lost Empire, the queue stretching back between Puffing Demons and Airships. Ellie watched as some of the antique cars puttered by, sending gouts of steam into the air as they earned their name.

Ellie, Cole, and the Taters followed two switchbacks before the façade for the house came into view. Still in the theme of the land, a broken stone wall with dried and stained skeletons on either side greeted the guests as torn white sheets fluttered in the breeze. Ellie still hadn't walked through Undead Empire since it was finished, and she was excited to see what Kevin and

Gus had come up with. It was an odd pairing for the design, but they were the biggest zombie fans in the park.

She'd heard from Capy that the finished house was gorier than what Ellie had seen during construction, but still not as bad as Carnival Carnage.

There were no subtle notes of esoteric music here. A heavy metal riff and double kick drums assaulted them as soon as they reached the entrance. Someone grabbed her arm, and she found Tottie sidled up against her.

"You're going first, right? I hate zombies, Ellie. Hate them!"

Part of Ellie felt bad for dragging Tottie to a zombie house. Another part of her thought Poe was about to be extremely happy with their footage.

"I'll go first with Cole. You hang back a bit, okay?"

Tottie nodded rapidly and walked behind them, Poe trailing her with the camera.

A dimly lit, rusted sign greeted them. *Go Back. City Lost.* Shadows moved all along the wall, some meant to be the flickering of torches, while others had a more human shape, but at least one was something else entirely.

Ellie stared at the shadowed hallway when the groans started, hesitating when a pair of golden glowing eyes reflected the light. The audio track for the house kicked in, a fast conversation between two people.

"Look for the eyes! They'll reflect the light."

"What if I don't have any light?"

"Stay with me. We'll get through this."

Every light in the room blacked out. Ellie jumped at a crash of cymbals. Tottie shrieked when the lights flickered back on, and the sunken face of a cadaverous zombie shambled just beside them. He must have leapt forward while the lights were dimmed, but he moved slowly now.

"Look for the eyes," echoed around them as they entered the far hallway.

On cue, as the vocal track faded, eyes appeared along the wall, some clearly projections, some most assuredly not. And something else reached them, the distant stench of rot as though a neighbor had left fishbones in the trash too long.

"Oh, nasty," Cole shouted over the pounding soundtrack.

The second room opened around them, the illusion of cobblestones and an ancient gas streetlamp to their left. A boarded-up building waited to the right, and the path curved to its entrance, where the barricade had been ripped away.

Deep gouges shone in the brick, dripping something viscous in regular beats. The only warning the guests had was the clunk of a foot trigger when a break in the music dropped around them. A looming form roared as it stepped forward, the pale gray face of something not-quite human rushing them. Long arms reached ahead before it dove.

Ellie cringed away, but the scare actor vanished into the floor, disappearing in a curl of fog as if they'd never been there.

"That was amazing!" Poe shouted as the throbbing beats of metal pulsed through the room again.

A few more steps took them inside the building, destruction all around. The subtle decline of the floor gave the illusion they were on a long ramp into the underground, dodging fallen stone and timber as they went. Water joined the sounds nearby, the roar of a river deep within the earth.

Shadows raced across the ceiling, their true forms invisible except for the eyes. The vocal track whispered through the air.

"They aren't human anymore. They're something else now."

The click of a flashlight turned a solid beam onto the ceiling, and Ellie screamed as something swooped down. Too many eyes, too many arms, and it moved far too fast to be a zombie. It grabbed a guest out of line and disappeared into the darkness.

"What? What!" Tottie screamed. "Get me out of here!"

Ellie continued forward, trying to understand what had just happened. Nothing made sense. Roman wouldn't let the guests be touched in line. Something was wrong. Something was very wrong. She plunged ahead into the next hall, almost missing the scares completely as the boo holes opened and insect-like limbs lunged into her path.

The last room was a horde, a shambling mass of scare actors, some on stilts, and simple animatronics that filled the entire place with a gory diorama of death. It would have been impressive, even amazing, if Ellie hadn't been panicked and racing through it.

She shot through the exit with Cole and the Taters close behind, and came face to face with Kevin, her words tumbling out. "They took a guest!"

He roared with laughter.

Ellie stared at him in confusion. "Have you lost it? We could get shut down!"

Kevin wiped at his eyes, almost hyperventilating, as the others followed Ellie out of the house. "No, Ellie. That was Gus. He's one of the plants for the walkthroughs. You didn't even notice him slip in after the first blackout, did you?"

Ellie blinked. Then let out a long, relieved sigh. "Kevin. I'm going to kill you as soon as I kill Gus."

"Yes! That's exactly the reaction we're hoping for. I'll tell him you approve." Kevin nodded to the others. "What did you all think? Favorite house this year on *Taters' Rides and Guides*?"

"It's up there," Poe said.

Tottie shook her head. "I don't need to smell that house again." She paused. "Great job, though. I mean, they got me a few times."

Cole patted Kevin's shoulder. "Tell Gus to keep it up. I knew it was coming, and it still freaked me out."

"You *knew*?" Ellie glared at Cole.

"I didn't want to ruin your first trip through!"

The Taters burst into laughter.

Chapter 24

"GINGERBREAD CAKE WITH gingerbread buttercream icing and stuffed with gingerbread whipped cream!" Ellie bounced on her heels and held the little round cake out to Cole.

"Good thing I'm not allergic to ginger." He eyed the snack with some suspicion.

Some of Ellie's favorite events were when the park was closed, and only those who lived there or wanted to stay after hours remained. She grabbed her own tray and moved down the line, enjoying the haphazard stacks and lack of organization that had gone into the buffet. Dessert sat next to breakfast, which waited beside peppermint coffee and hot cocoa, which in turn bordered dishes of breakfast tots, complete with eggs, bacon, and a river of melted white cheese.

They sat down at a table close to the buffet on the far side of the café. Ellie made it halfway through the tots in all their greasy, cheesy glory before she noticed Cole hadn't touched his cake. "You have to eat that before it melts."

"You need to help me eat that, Ellie. There's no way I can take all of this down."

"I have faith in you."

Cole snorted a laugh and pushed the cake toward Ellie. "It might be dinnertime, but I need to rebuild my appetite."

She grinned at him, cut a slice off with her fork, and tried it. It wasn't the lightest cake by any means, but the slight chew was a nice texture. The burst of ginger felt like a warm hug even as the filling washed some of it away. Ellie tried the buttercream on its own, sighed, and then took a bite with every layer in it.

"It's perfect. It just tastes like the holidays."

Cole reached out with his fork and cut a piece off, taking a tentative bite before pursing his lips. "It's not bad, but it's so sweet."

"You're going to suck down an entire cut comb milkshake and then call *this* sweet? I mean, it *is* sweet, but it's not *that* sweet."

"You definitely need more sugar, Ellie."

She stuck her tongue out at him and took a huge bite of cake. "Good idea. You're coming with me to look at the decorations tonight, right?"

"I said I would." Cole's enthusiasm made it sound like she'd asked him to help squeegee Merrows Lagoon by hand.

Ellie knew Cole didn't have the best memories around the holidays, but she did. When her parents were still alive, they'd always had a Christmas tree in their living room. The in-laws on her mom's side celebrated Hanukkah, and her dad's side of the family had generally just crossed their fingers that *any* holiday festivities would be canceled. Ellie didn't think you'd lived until you'd had a leftover ham and cheesy potato casserole sandwich on slightly stale Challah bread.

She wasn't sure if she liked the flavor more, or the look of horror everyone in the family gave her when she ate it. It had been a long time since those days. Before everything changed. She shook herself from that train of thought.

"Didn't you ever celebrate the solstice in Faerie?" Ellie took another bite of cake. "Roman told me a lot of our traditions came from that."

"It wasn't always nice, Ellie." Cole looked away for a moment before continuing. "If you weren't … for the changelings, I mean. We weren't looked on highly if we hadn't sent humans back to Faerie. I don't … I don't have a lot of good memories."

She pushed the cake a little closer to Cole. "Let's try to make some new ones, maybe. For both of us."

"I'd like that." He stabbed the cake and took a larger bite. "And I have to admit, this cake is pretty good, too."

With their meal finished, Ellie and Cole set out into the park, heading through the Dark Forest so they could reach the main walkway. That was the quickest way back to Titania's Table, and Ellie didn't want to miss the tree lighting.

Even the Dark Forest had decorations up, but they were mostly themed to the Midwest. Glittery pine cones and jars of acorns hung along the walkways, winding between bright white lights and rusted metal sleighs. It felt festive and fit the theme of the land all at the same time.

In the central hub, the tree couldn't be missed. Almost as tall as Thrud and Yngvarr, the dying conifer had been rejuvenated by the Fae, a tradition Roman didn't speak about at length. But he said it was far older than any human tradition when it came to decorating a tree.

The pine tree's branches swept upward, its trunk set into the ground and already rooted thanks to the same magic that had revived it. Gus hopped from branch to branch, adding the final touches to the broad crown, a string of acorns and unadorned pine cones to complement those already hanging from the branches.

Robins and wrens perched throughout the branches, their simple animatronics turning their heads from time to time. Roman pulled the tree skirt back and plugged a heavy cord into a concealed outlet.

The older Fae looked up at the tree. "We are ready when you are, Gus."

Gus tied off the end of the garland and dropped through the branches until he landed beside Roman with a thud. "Ready!"

Ellie reached out and took Cole's hand, lacing her fingers between the warmth of his.

"Wendy, would you do the honors?" Roman gestured to a switch at the corner of the building.

Wendy eyed Nessa, who was double-checking the wiring. "No shocks this year?"

Nessa shook her head. "No shocks. You're all set."

Wendy turned back to Roman. "I'd love to. Thank you. I can't remember the last time I had a proper Yule celebration. I do hope you have mincemeat on the menu this year."

"You'll have to speak with Hans and Franzi regarding that."

Wendy smiled, reached out with her trunk, and threw the switch.

Warm white light bloomed from the tree, catching on sparkling snowflakes as they twisted between the branches. The garland formed a sweeping pattern from the boughs to the crown, overlapping in a way Ellie hadn't noticed without the lights.

"Wow." Cole squeezed her hand. "You know, that looks pretty good."

The low plucked notes of a lute filled the courtyard, a familiar tune, but one Ellie couldn't quite place. As though it was a song passed down through the ages, changing with every musician who made it their own.

"Should we sing, bro?" Manfred asked.

Roman slowly raised an eyebrow and studied the shretma. "If you wish."

"After this song, bro! Tradition is good, but I like the metal."

Ellie grinned at the dour expression on Roman's face.

"When the old songs are done, Manfred, you may do as you wish."

Manfred leaned toward Katinka, whispering quite loudly. "Like twenty minutes max, bro. Then we rock this place."

Cole laughed and pulled Ellie closer. She smiled at the twinkling snowflakes in the Yule tree. It was an old tradition. Certainly older than the Christmas tree her family had, but a common thread that bound them all together through the ages.

The dancing notes of the lute quieted, and Hans stepped forward. "Eggnog is ready! Come get yours in Lost Empire. And we have alcohol-free nog, too, Ellie."

She pulled on Cole's arm. "Come on. I've never had eggnog!"

"I don't know if that's a bad thing," Cole muttered as she dragged him across the courtyard, headed to the central path.

They walked past Treasures of Valhalla, the retail shop in Howling Mountain, now dripping in garland that had tiny yetis hidden in it, held up by a troll in a Santa hat. Soon enough, they crossed into Lost Empire, the garland there more like twigs and bare branches bound together with occasional bursts of green pine needles, and deep amber lights.

It fit the land and still felt festive. Ellie smiled when she caught Cole's expression. He was clearly more than a little impressed with the décor.

"I really thought this wasn't going to look as good as the other lands when I saw it during the day." He glanced from one side of the path to the other. "They did a great job with it, though."

"They really did, didn't they?"

Ellie hurried to the takeout window, where a large sign carved to look like a mug had a list of eggnogs to pick from. Most of them had whiskey or rum or some other alcohol, but two at the bottom didn't.

"What do you want to try?" Franzi asked, her whiskers twitching.

"Butterscotch eggnog, please!"

Cole winced. "Is that as sweet as it sounds, Franzi?"

"Oh, yes. It's wonderful."

Hans huffed and puffed as he walked in behind Franzi. "The kids are fast."

"No, we aren't," Ellie said. "We just left before you."

Franzi shook her head. "No, no, he's just getting old." She cut Hans off before he could respond. "What kind would you like, Cole?"

"I'll go for the traditional flavor on the kids menu."

Franzi chuckled at that. "Kids menu. I like it."

"You didn't ask," Hans said.

"Hans, we know them. We don't need to ask the question."

"We ask everyone."

Franzi sighed as she shook the eggnog in a metal tin with

one paw. "Do either of you have an egg allergy?"

"No," they chorused.

"Thank you, Franzi," Hans said.

She smiled at the other slibreg before pouring the shaker into a moose cup, poking the bottom with a claw to turn on the flasher.

"Blinky cups!" Ellie bounced on her heels. "Poe's going to be so excited."

Franzi flipped the shaker and dropped a similar set of ingredients into it before shaking it with a flourish and pouring it into another moose cup. "And the traditional."

"Thanks, Franzi!" Ellie held her cup out to Cole. "Cheers."

They clinked blinky cups and took a sip of the cold eggnog.

Ellie frowned as she swirled it across her tongue. Certainly thicker than she'd expected, but so creamy and rich. "The nutmeg and cinnamon! This is fantastic. Oh, and the butterscotch notes."

Cole sipped at his and shrugged. "Well, it's eggnog."

Franzi slapped a paw on the counter. "Hans, we have our new slogan. Put it in lights. Order the neon sign. *Well, It's Eggnog.*"

Ellie snorted a laugh and stepped back as some of the other Fae caught up to them. "Try this one, Cole." They switched mugs, and she took a sip of his traditional eggnog. It wasn't as sweet as the butterscotch, but still had that amazing texture with the cinnamon and nutmeg notes. "I love eggnog, I think."

Cole held the blinky cup out to switch back. "I changed my mind. The original is fantastic. Yours is like chewing on a butterscotch caramel. Or maybe drowning in butterscotch caramel."

"So good," Ellie whispered. "Come on, Cole. We have an hour before dinner. Let's go look at the rest of the decorations."

"As long as they aren't butterscotch."

Ellie grinned at him.

AFTER A QUICK run by their apartments to drop off the rather awkward blinky cups, Ellie and Cole made their way back through Howling Mountain. Odin's Hall had a massive log burning in a fire pit outside, casting shapes and shadows all around the holly-decked timbers of the building itself.

They stayed on the trail to the Bobsled and followed the walking path into Carnival. Nothing had quite prepared Ellie for the onslaught of chaos that waited in that land. Kitschy antique Christmas lights and plastic yard décor spread across every free inch of the place. Some of them bore nightmarish faces she assumed were supposed to be Santa Clauses, but age had not been kind to them.

"This is nuts," Cole said, looking around the land in awe.

Ellie pulled on his jacket. "Look! They put lights on the Bobsled!"

Multicolored flashing lights raced around the track, following the course the coaster would take when it ran. A plastic reindeer sat anchored near the top of the lift hill.

Ellie snorted as they passed the pretzel stand, seeing the utter madness of the carnival games. Lighted penguins and holiday gnomes, ceramic trees, and glittering presents, and even an ugly, illuminated cow camped out atop Balloon Darts.

"Who did this?" Ellie asked with a laugh.

"I'm pretty sure this land was all Manfred and Katinka."

Cole gestured to the Santa with a Flying V guitar strapped to his chest.

"Oh, that makes a lot of sense. I can't wait to hear the music they picked. Let's get back to the—"

Ellie didn't get to finish before the distorted slide of a guitar screeched through Carnival. Heavy growls and screams started up, and it took a moment for her to recognize Greensleeves.

"I don't recognize these lyrics." Cole frowned. "What is this?"

"You're thinking of 'What Child is This?'"

"Yes, exactly."

"Well, that song was a rewrite of *this* song. It's called 'Greensleeves.' But I don't think I've ever heard a heavy metal version before." Ellie laughed and grabbed Cole's hand. "Come on, let's go get dinner."

ELLIE SAT IN the garden at Titania's Table with Roman, Cole, Capy, Bruce, and a handful of other brave Fae. The rest of them planned to eat inside, away from the garden, and—as many of them hoped—away from Titania's gaze. The bass from Manfred's metal symphony still resonated in the distance, but the music in the garden was considerably quieter.

"Please remain seated, everyone." Roman stood at the head of the table, a long rectangular thing that had replaced the cluster of round tables from Halloween. A cloth hid the steaming food from prying eyes, only piquing Ellie's curiosity. All eyes focused on Roman.

"I would like to say a few words before we begin, though I will keep it short, as the work of Hans, Franzi, and their team should not be allowed to cool. This has been an outstanding year, both for the park and in developments I thought might never come to Faerie.

"It has not gone unnoticed, even in my absence, the level you each have dedicated yourselves to this park. And I say this to those of you inside as well."

Ellie glanced toward the restaurant, finding a cluster of faces peering out the open doors to listen to Roman.

"It has been years since I celebrated Yule. The first year this park was open. Not so long ago to many of us Fae, but before that … I cannot recall. The war stole from many of us. The aftermath brought us together. I am glad to spend this time with you all. Old friends and new, old family and new." He tipped his hat to Ellie.

"So, thank you, all who dwell and work here. I take your gratitude without debt and give you my own. To brighter times, when the sun returns." Roman raised his glass. "Let us feast!"

The cloth over the food vanished, taking with it a curl of steam from the warmest dishes. Miniature duck galette, roasted potatoes and squash, opaque bottles of mead, mince pies and trifles, cranberry sauce, and brussels sprouts. Sprouts were something Ellie had loathed until Roman introduced her to a charred version of the dish. A dash of ranch dressing, and she adored them.

Ellie gestured to the slibreg at the far side of the table. "Hans, Franzi, this looks amazing."

"Wait until you taste it," Hans said, baring his long front teeth in a grin.

"We don't have any serving utensils," Cole said. "I'm guessing we aren't supposed to pick these up off the trays."

"Ah, of course." Roman held his fingers out and snapped.

From one instant to the next, the food swapped from the serving trays to the plates in front of every seat at the table. Judging by the impressed noises coming from inside, he'd done the same for everyone at the celebration.

Ellie snatched up the galette first. Duck was another dish she'd never had before her time with Fae. She started to take a bite before her gaze fell on Bruce. "Is … is this weird?"

Bruce frowned, then laughed. "I'm a weregoose, Ellie, not a wereduck." It wasn't exactly the most explanatory answer, but when Bruce took a bit of galette himself, she figured she was in the clear.

The pastry broke into individual layers as she bit into it, buttery squash and winter seasonings exploding across her tongue. "Eat. The. Duck." She hissed the words at Cole. It was tender, juicy, with an amazing fatty flavor that set it apart from chicken.

"This might be the best thing I've ever eaten." Cole eyed the galette in his hand.

Ellie moved on to the roasted potatoes, crisp and bright with fresh rosemary and notes of citrus in the butter. One after another, the slibregs' dishes were some of the best food she'd ever had.

"My friends." Roman opened his arms to Hans and Franzi. "You have truly outdone yourselves. A meal fit for the grandest halls of Faerie."

Franzi's nose twitched. "Wait until you try dessert." She raised a steaming mug of mead and tipped it toward Roman.

*

ELLIE DIDN'T UNDERSTAND how she could have possibly eaten so much but didn't feel miserable. She wouldn't have been surprised if one of the Fae had enchanted the food to exactly that effect, but it wasn't something she was worried about in the moment. It didn't stop her from walking out with a couple snickerdoodles in tow.

One thing was certain. "We need to get some sleep before first shift tomorrow."

Cole groaned. "Don't remind me. I have a double."

"Me, too. Fae hours and cleanup." She sighed and leaned against Cole. "Helping cover the new vacation schedule for the brownies while HR trains the new hires. Bex should be happy."

They wandered in silence for a time, heading toward the apartments. It wasn't until they were standing in front of Ellie's home that Cole shuffled his feet, then reached out for a hug.

Ellie lightly held him back, grabbed his cheeks, and placed a long, soft kiss on his lips. "Have a good night, Cole."

Cole paused before rambling a question out almost faster than Ellie could follow. "I was wondering if you might want to go to the movies?"

"Sure!" She didn't hesitate for even a moment. "What did you want to see? I think the new one about a sentient cactus who battles space dinosaurs is coming out this week."

Cole blinked. "I was thinking something more, like … well, I was thinking something more like a date movie."

Ellie paused with a snickerdoodle in her mouth. She chewed and swallowed before nodding. "That sounds great, Cole. I'd love to. But can we do something afterward where we can actually talk? I love movies, but you know, talking is generally frowned at."

"Definitely!" Cole perked up. "I have a couple ideas, if you'd like to pick?"

Ellie shook her head and smiled. "Surprise me."

Also by Eric R. Asher

Shop ebooks, audiobooks, and paperbacks at
ericrasherstore.com

The Theme Park at the End of the World

The Steamborn Series

Steamborn

Steamforged

Steamsworn

Skyborn

Skyforged

Skysworn

Stormborn

Stormforged

Stormsworn

The Vesik Series
(Recommended for Ages 17+)

Days Gone Bad

Wolves and the River of Stone

Winter's Demon

This Broken World

Destroyer Rising

Rattle the Bones

Witch Queen's War

Forgotten Ghosts

The Book of the Ghost

The Book of the Claw

The Book of the Sea
The Book of the Staff
The Book of the Rune
The Book of the Sails
The Book of the Wing
The Book of the Blade
The Book of the Fang
The Book of the Reaper
Dreams of the Forgotten Dead
Garden Gnome Graves

The Vesik Series Box Sets

Box Set One (Books 1-3)
Box Set Two (Books 4-6)
Box Set Three (Books 7-8)
Box Set Four: The Books of the Dead Part 1
Box Set Five: The Books of the Dead Part 2

Mason Dixon: Monster Hunter

Episode One
Episode Two
Episode Three
Episode Four

Want to receive an email when one of Eric's books releases?
Visit ericrasher.com to get started.

About the Author

Eric is a former bookseller, cellist, and comic seller currently living in Saint Louis, Missouri. A lifelong enthusiast of books, music, toys, and games, he discovered a love for the written word after being dragged to the library by his parents at a young age. When he is not writing, you can usually find him reading, gaming, or buried beneath a small avalanche of Transformers. For more about Eric, see: www.ericrasher.com

Enjoy this book? You can make a big difference.

If you've enjoyed this book, I would be very grateful if you could take a minute to leave a review on the platform of your choice. It can be as short as you like. Thank you for spending time with Ellie and Cole.

Connect with Eric R. Asher Online:

Facebook: @ericrasher

Instagram: @ericrasher

TikTok: ericrasher

ericrasher.com

ericrasherstore.com

www.ingramcontent.com/pod-product-compliance
Lightning Source LLC
Chambersburg PA
CBHW032246310726
48973CB00008B/2311